A Visit
to Highbury

Also by Joan Austen-Leigh

Stephanie
Stephanie at War

PLAYS (Joan Mason Hurley)
Our Own Particular Jane
Canadian One Act Plays for Women
Four Canadian One Act Plays
Women and Love
Women's Work

A Visit to Highbury

Joan Austen-Leigh

St. Martin's Press
New York

ISBN 0-312-11860-0

First published in Canada under the title *Mrs. Goddard, Mistress of
a School* by A Room of One's Own Press

First U.S. Edition: March 1995
10 9 8 7 6 5 4 3 2 1

J. David Grey
very dear friend
who greatly enriched my life

ACKNOWLEDGEMENT

This has been an enterprise not lightly undertaken. Any attempt such as this is likely to invite both disaster and disdain.

Nevertheless, kind friends and colleagues have graciously read all or part of the manuscript and have been most helpful in their advice and criticism. I was thus saved from making many egregious errors; any that remain – and someone is bound to discover them – must be accounted my responsibility. My very sincere thanks to: Tibbie Adams, Damaris Brix, Juliet McMaster, Bruce Stovell, Eileen Sutherland and the late J. David Grey.

I am most grateful to the Jane Austen Society of North America for awarding me a Henry G. Burke grant to assist in the publication of this book.

J A-L

PREFACE

This story is for those who love *Emma*.

Readers like myself, who consider the words and characters of Jane Austen sacrosanct, may rest assured that it is with the utmost fidelity to the original that I have constructed this tale.

In viewing life in Highbury through Mrs. Goddard's eyes, I have not altered a single fact, circumstance or detail of Jane Austen's masterpiece.

My characters do not intrude upon hers, nor have I presumed to put words in the mouths of any of Jane Austen's people. Those who speak in *Emma*, speak only indirectly here. Those who are silent in *Emma*, I have encouraged to talk to Mrs. Goddard. In addition, I have tried, with a few exceptions, to use no word that was not used by J.A.

In dating the letters between Mrs. Goddard and her sister, I have adhered strictly to the chronology of *Emma* as traced by R. W. Chapman and Jo Modert – though, like Frank Churchill arranging to sit next to Emma at the Coles' dinner, it has been "not without some contrivance" on my part.

JOAN AUSTEN-LEIGH
great-great-great-niece of Jane Austen

"The post-office is a wonderful establishment!" said she. – "The regularity and despatch of it! If one thinks of all that it has to do, and all that it does so well, it is really astonishing."

From *Emma*

CAST OF CHARACTERS

Mrs. Goddard was the mistress of a School – not of a seminary, or an establishment, or any thing which professed, in long sentences of refined nonsense, to combine liberal acquirements with elegant morality upon new principles and new systems – and where young ladies for enormous pay might be screwed out of health and into vanity – but a real, honest, old-fashioned Boarding-school, where a reasonable quantity of accomplishments were sold at a reasonable price, and where girls might be sent to be out of the way and scramble themselves into a little education, without any danger of coming back prodigies. Mrs. Goddard's school was in high repute – and very deservedly; for Highbury was reckoned a particularly healthy spot: she had an ample house and garden, gave the children plenty of wholesome food, let them run about a great deal in the summer, and in winter dressed their chilblains with her own hands. It was no wonder that a train of twenty young couple now walked after her to church. She was a plain, motherly kind of woman, who had worked hard in her youth, and now thought herself entitled to the occasional holiday of a tea-visit; and having formerly owed much to Mr. Woodhouse's kindness, felt his particular claim on her to leave her neat parlour hung round with fancy-work whenever she could, and win or lose a few sixpences by his fireside.

FROM *Emma*

LETTER 1

From Mrs. Goddard to Mrs. Pinkney

The School,
Highbury, Surry
3 October 1813

My dear Charlotte,

Your dejected letter of yesterday has just come. Well, of course I very much regret on my own account that your visit to Highbury must again be deferred: I blame myself that in my great desire to see you, and knowing that you were *now* only sixteen miles away, I encouraged the scheme. Really, it was a very selfish and unreasonable one. So short a time as you have been married, it was not to be supposed that your husband would willingly part with you. We ought each of us to have considered what was due to Mr. Pinkney.

Small comfort these words, I realize, and I beg your pardon if I verge on delivering a homily. It is a failing among elder sisters that they tend to advise and admonish younger ones, especially when the elder sister happens to be the mistress of a school! Believe me, I am quite as disappointed as you are, but to look on the bright side, I must have neglected you had you come now, at the beginning of the school year, when I have so much on my hands. Later, when the new girls have settled in and everything is in a regular train, I shall be more at leisure to enjoy your society. Perhaps near Christmas, or in the spring, Mr. Pinkney may spare you, at least for two or three days.

Alas, I cannot suggest your bringing him with you. I am sure a former Cambridge don would find it very awkward to be staying in a girls' school; a far cry from high table in hall, even if a spare bedchamber could be found. I am sorry to say that the local inn, the Crown, is quite out of the question; dirty wall paper and yellowing paint. "Inconsiderable" is the only word to describe it.

Meantime, we must console ourselves with this nice little correspondence in which you seem more ready to engage than formerly. You cannot write too often to please me. Though for my part, I fear that Highbury does not in general supply any very sensational news. This week, however, has been an exception. The truly amiable Miss Taylor, governess at Hartfield, was married to the general favourite, Mr. Weston of Randalls.

I suppose I am a romantic at heart, and feel that a happy marriage should be the ultimate goal of every young – or, in Miss Taylor's case, not so young – woman. Certainly I always rejoice whenever I hear of the weddings of any of my former pupils.

In this instance, everyone is delighted at Miss Taylor's good fortune. Everyone, that is, except dear old Mr. Woodhouse, her former employer. He speaks in a mournful voice of "poor Miss Taylor," as if the good lady were *dead*! Dear silly old man. You have to know and love him to understand and overlook his idiosyncracies.

But enough. I will not bore you with further particulars. I know our affairs at Highbury are of very little interest outside our own circle. What is most important at the moment is *you*. Dear Charlotte, let me hear that you are happy and well-settled into your new life in London.

My compliments to Mr. Pinkney. One day, before too long I hope, we shall become acquainted.

Your affectionate sister,
M. Goddard

LETTER 2

From Mrs. Pinkney to Mrs. Goddard

Sloane Street,
London
6 October 1813

Do not speak to me of truly amiable women marrying general favourites of men, my dear Mary. It is not a subject I find congenial.

No. I am not, I cannot, I will not be resigned.

That two sisters who have not seen each other for so many years should be by *him* kept apart provokes me every hour of every day. When I resided in Yorkshire I knew it was impossible that we should meet. But now, to be separated by a mere sixteen miles is more than flesh and blood can bear.

I do not accept your statement that we should have considered what was due to Mr. Pinkney. *Nothing* is due to him; no more than if I were his housekeeper requesting a few days leave of absence. For as a housekeeper am I treated, and as such, I believe, he married me.

Who would have thought that in consenting to become Mrs. Pinkney my life would undergo such a change for the worse? *He* sits all day in his study; *I* sit all alone in the drawing room. I think I shall go mad!

When I tire of looking out of the window, I turn for solace to the pages of a book. When I was married to Mr. Grenville, I had no more time for reading than for writing. Now I am deep in the *Romance of the Forest*, which I never happened to have read before. What delightful shivers run down one's spine as Adeline, her candle guttering, pushes open the secret door in her chamber! But you are despising my taste, I feel sure. *You* never sink to Mrs.

Radcliffe. *You*, no doubt, still read only improving books. But I confess I do love a mystery, and its solving in the last few pages is quite delightful to me. I wish you had any mysteries at Highbury. If you had, I might exercise my wits by correspondence.

Oh, yes, I do most humbly concede that I have been a sad writer of letters these last few years, and have not appeared to take the interest in your affairs at Highbury that my affection for you should warrant. What can I say in my defence? Only that Mr. Grenville was so demanding of my attention and so much of my time was given over to entertaining our friends and providing good meals – for you know how sociable he was and *needed* to be as a successful attorney – that I had little inclination to sit at my desk and apply myself to my pen. Now, your letters are my sole salvation, my only contact with rational, normal, happy people.

Give me another set of beings to think about. No detail shall be too wearisome, not even, if you must, "poor Miss Taylor's" wedding. A profusion of white satin, was there? Many guests? Barrels of oysters? Flagons of wine? Tell me.

Your miserable sister,
Charlotte Pinkney

LETTER 3

From Mrs. Goddard to Mrs. Pinkney

The School,
Highbury, Surry
9 October 1813

My dear Charlotte,

I am excessively distressed and shocked. Why are you no better than a housekeeper? Why do you each sit in a separate room? What do you mean by saying you will go mad? I do not understand. Was not Mr. Pinkney one of Mr. Grenville's oldest friends? I know it was not a match of affection. But surely, surely, when you consented to the marriage at least you had some regard and respect?

You make me very unhappy indeed and I find it almost impossible to write the sort of letter you ask for when my spirits are so oppressed with concern for you. Do make an effort, my dear, for Mr. Pinkney's sake as well as your own. I cannot believe he married you merely to get a housekeeper. What grounds do you have for such a charge?

Later: I was called away by Miss Nash to arbitrate between two of the girls over a missing French exercise book. Peace is now restored. Would that matters between you and Mr. Pinkney could be as easily mended.

Well, I shall try, in spite of my heavy heart, to comply with your request, though I confess to being somewhat astonished. You have never expressed much interest in Highbury before. But if you really think that cheerful news will lift up your spirits – though about people whom you have never met, I will make the attempt; and hope it is of service. Since my thoughts are still full of Miss Taylor's wedding, if you can endure to hear of it, I shall begin with that.

I believe Emma Woodhouse was instrumental in encouraging the match for she was often inviting Mr. Weston to Hartfield, where he was very warmly welcomed, being a gentleman of most pleasant manners. Poor old Mr. Woodhouse had no suspicion that his hospitality would be repaid by the removal from under his roof of a charming and much-loved friend and companion. He is quite opposed to change of any kind, and abhors match-making and weddings. I have often heard him at the card table express disapproval of matches for they "break up one's family circle grievously". It is of no use to point out to him that without matches and marriages there would be no family circles!

I cannot give you particulars of the actual ceremony. I suppose it was in deference to Mr. Woodhouse's nerves that none of us in Highbury, who might count ourselves old friends, were invited. Present were only, Mr. Woodhouse and Emma, one of Mr. Weston's brothers from town and two or three old servants.

Even Mr. Knightley, owner of Donwell Abbey and a devoted friend of the family, was absent – visiting his brother in town. I have mentioned before, only you probably do not remember, that Mr. John Knightley of Brunswick Square is married to Emma's elder sister, Isabella. I was a little surprised that *she*, to whom Miss Taylor was also governess, did not make the effort to come down from London for such a very special occasion.

Here at the school, my three teachers and I each received a piece of wedding cake. Very good of Mrs. Weston to remember us. It was made by Serle at Hartfield and was wonderfully rich and delicious, with generous quantities of currants and brandy. This was all much against the wishes of Mr. Woodhouse, you understand. In his opinion wedding cake is most unwholesome and injurious to the digestion.

The happy couple's hands were joined in matrimony by Mr. Elton, a superior young man who has lived alone at the Vicarage for the past year, and whose every movement is a source of absorbing interest to all the single young ladies of Highbury including the girls and teachers in this school. Perhaps *his* betrothal will be next; though who in Highbury he would deem good enough to be his consort I cannot imagine.

Since the wedding Mrs. Weston is often to be seen driving about in her carriage with her pleasant husband at her side. Never did a woman look happier. I well remember when, as Miss Taylor, she first arrived in Highbury to take over the two motherless little girls at Hartfield. I had not been long here myself at the time. I was reckoning up only the other day: sixteen years has she been with Mr. Woodhouse. So I suppose she must be nearly forty or thereabouts. How one hopes that it is not too late, for I am sure that a child would be the greatest joy to her.

Mr. Weston, of course, already has a son. He lives at Enscombe in Yorkshire, adopted by rich relatives of the first wife. He is very proud of this young man and sees him every year in London. To us in Highbury, however, Frank is almost a myth, since he has never come near the place since his mother died. But we live in hopes. He wrote a very handsome letter to Miss Taylor; and a wedding visit to his father is promised.

There! I hope you have not found this account of life in Highbury too tedious since it cost me a good deal of effort to write. If you wish to hear from me more frequently, I am afraid you must put up with the same subject, because I have no other.

Now I must leave off. It is time for evening prayers. Tonight my text is from *Proverbs*, Chapter 31, verses 10 & 11. I am sure you remember the passage. It was one of my Father's favourites, and most instructive and suitable for girls.

Dear Charlotte, I am thinking of you constantly with concern and alarm. Please write soon and give me a better account of yourself and Mr. Pinkney.

Goodbye and God bless you,
M. Goddard

P.S. Indeed, I do not read improving books now. With over forty young ladies under my care, as well as all the teachers, servants and management of the school to oversee, I have no time for reading anything. I think I may say that my only relaxation is the occasional evening visit to Mr. Woodhouse.

LETTER 4

From Mrs. Pinkney to Mrs. Goddard

Sloane Street,
London
12 October 1813

My dear Mary,

Yes, I remember that text only too well. "Who can find a virtuous woman, for her price is far above rubies?" I suppose Miss Taylor is virtuous. She certainly is fortunate to have found, at her time of life, such a suitable husband, especially after so many years spent as a governess, *and* in such a small place as Highbury. With all my heart I wish her happy. Heaven knows it is not always that a marriage in later life proves to be so.

Oh, what a mistake I have made in marrying Mr. Pinkney! If only I had accepted your offer after Mr. Grenville died and had come to assist you at your school. How infinitely preferable it would have been to this, my present wretched situation; but having never had children myself, I was in doubt if my nerves at the age of forty-two would be equal to the pandemonium. Now, I am persuaded that noise would be delightful *indeed* compared to the deathly quiet which surrounds me, where the only sounds to be heard are the ticking of the clock and the distant footsteps of the servants.

If you are willing, my refuge shall be this correspondence. Your news from Highbury shall bring a beam of sunshine into this gloomy house, into which I bitterly regret that I ever set foot. When I think of my previous neglect of you, I am thoroughly ashamed. My present intention is positively to inundate you with letters, though Heavens knows what I can write about. To all my other miseries is now added *gout*. Mr. P.'s foot is much swollen, and naturally this affliction does not improve his disposition or matters between us.

As I sit alone brooding, I reflect on the dear old days in Yorkshire. With a total want of concern for the future did Mr. Grenville and I eat, drink, and career about in our carriage. Debts and extravagance, and joyful times! We thought the fountain would never run dry. Good Lord, when I think of the excellent income he used to earn and how barely a brass farthing now remains, I am mortified indeed.

Only twice as I had met Mr. P. before the funeral, he appeared to be a reasonable, scholarly gentleman. He wanted a wife, and I needed a husband. It seemed likely to be a satisfactory arrangement. I presumed that the pleasures of London would compensate me for the lack of affection and the loss of my friends in Yorkshire. Besides, I was escaping from the prospect of poverty and having to live in lodgings above a shop, or some such squalid habitation.

But in the process of settling into this dark and sunless house – which I would never have chosen – many little domestic matters and disagreements served to divide us. My expectations were, I now conclude, unreasonable. I should have foreseen that Mr. P., having been all his life a bachelor, would vary his regimen not in the slightest particular to accommodate a wife. Still, I did presume that the ordinary civilities of two people living under the same roof would be observed. But I was mistaken. He goes twice a week to the whist club, otherwise he remains shut up in his room reading, or studying chess moves on a board when his friend, Mr. Fowler, a horrible, wizened old clergyman with a yellow face and a cackling laugh, is not available to play with him. Since he seldom goes from home on any social occasion where ladies are present, I have no alternative but to remain incarcerated within doors. I might as well be in prison.

My dearest Mary, my pen has run away with me and I can feel your displeasure. You never approved of complainers. But I can keep up the pretence of a successful alliance no longer.

Before you throw this letter down in disgust, let me tell you something that is *not* a complaint, and which – being in the same line of business – I think will amuse you. Can you believe that we actually live next door to a girls' school?

They have only just returned from the summer holidays, otherwise I would have discovered this before. My chief entertainment is to sit in the bow window of the drawing-room, where I can observe the activity in the street: the carriages, the muffin men, the sedan chairs, etc., but the single most interesting sight, by far, is the comings and goings of the young ladies of this school: or seminary, perhaps I should say, since it is one of the first in the town, Betty tells me. She knows the parlour maid employed there. Italian is taught as well as all the usual subjects and many additional accomplishments such as harp and violin, dancing and making screens. The girls are all very elegantly dressed, but look pale, poor things, and thin, not in the glowing health and overflowing spirits which I understand has ever been your care in your estimable establishment. Betty says the girls are often ill and the apothecary is forever having to be sent for. The place is run by a pseudo-Frenchwoman calling herself Madame Dubois. I believe she is no more French than we are, but gives herself a certain *cachet* by assuming this identity. Is this not amusing? Are you not interested to hear more? I shall let you know whatever else I may discover.

Speaking of discoveries, I have something to relate concerning your recent wedding in Highbury. Mr. Wingfield, the apothecary, was here to attend Mr. P. After he had seen my husband and prescribed for his gout, I invited him to take a dish of tea with me.

"It would be a kindness, sir," said I, "for I am newly-married and have no acquaintance in town; in general, I speak only to Mr. Pinkney and the servants from one day's end to another."

He looked surprised and with some reluctance sat down. He seemed not to converse easily, so after we had gone through the weather, to encourage him, I inquired if he had any special recommendations as to health.

"Yes, madam," said he, with increased enthusiasm. "I am a firm believer in the efficacy of sea-bathing."

"Sea-bathing!" cried I, astonished.

"In moderation, of course, and only in the warmer months. I particularly advise South End."

"South End? But I have heard that that is an unhealthy place, sir."

"No, indeed. My own brother and his family have been there repeatedly."

"You surprise me."

"I had the pleasure recently of recommending it to a family in Brunswick Square. They were there in September and found it answered extremely well. One of the little girls had been very much subject to sore throats."

"South End is quite forty miles from London," I observed, pricking up my ears at the mention of Brunswick Square. "They must be people of large means, sir?"

"No. The gentleman is a lawyer, but he considered the expense well worth it, for it did the children a vast deal of good."

"The lady has many children, sir?"

"Only five, at present," said he. "It is, however, usually an annual event. Sometimes Mrs. Knightley is a little over-concerned about their health, but the father is a sensible man."

I was highly amused, of course. Mr. Wingfield seemed unaware that he had mentioned a name. You would have been proud of me, my dear Mary, I did not betray by so much as a flicker of an eyelid that "Mrs. Knightley" meant anything in the world to me. Thus may I hope to discover more the next time he comes to call.

I hope you are suitably astonished. For is it not odd that though it seems we two sisters are not to meet, we have this connexion through strangers? At least *I* am not acquainted with the John Knightleys, and *you* do not know Mr. Wingfield. But I have been able to reveal – if you had any curiosity in the matter – a possible reason why they did not attend Miss Taylor's wedding. For all one knows it was too much to undertake so soon after their holiday? If you have any other mysteries you wish solved, pray address them to your sister.

By the way, what is the name of the young man, the "Frank," you spoke of as living at Enscombe in Yorkshire? A Mr. Weston, I presume?

I must conclude. Mr. P. requires me for his evening game of backgammon. He sits with his foot up upon a stool and is ordered to eat and drink less, which does not please him.

My dearest Mary, goodbye,
Charlotte Pinkney

P.S. Mr. Woodhouse sounds like an old misery. He and Mr. Pinkney would make a fine pair. Your evening visits to Hartfield must be excessively tedious.

From Mrs. Goddard to Mrs. Pinkney

Highbury,
18 October 1813

My school? Pandemonium! Certainly not. Cheerful bustle, if you please. It is just as well you did not come. I am persuaded it would not have suited you.

Now then, my dear Charlotte, I must speak to you seriously. I like not to hear you speak ill of your husband. I am excessively sorry that you are not happy, but you were not obliged to marry Mr. Pinkney, and I believe you owe him a debt of loyalty and gratitude whatever his faults of temper, which I daresay he cannot help, owing to his gout. I am told it is very painful, and it seems to me that what is required is sympathy and understanding on your part. The power of amendment is surely within your own hands? Think how much worse off you would have been had you remained in Yorkshire.

You must be well aware, with your lively temperament, that you have ever been subject to fluctuations of mood. For your own well-being and that of poor Mr. Pinkney, I beg you will make an effort. Surely he must be equally miserable? There now! I have relieved my mind of what I felt it to be my unpleasant duty to impart. Excuse me, my dear, if I exercise the prerogative of being your senior by five years, to give you this hint. You do not need to be told how much I have your welfare at heart.

Speaking of welfare, I was grieved rather than amused by what you had to tell me of the Seminary next door. I have heard of such places that charge enormous sums to turn healthy, natural girls into vain, affected, husband-hunting young women. Perfectly shocking. It ought not to be allowed.

Very diverting that Mr. Wingfield should be an unconscious link between Highbury and Sloane Street. I have often heard Mrs. Knightley speak of Mr. Wingfield. I know Mr. Woodhouse laments that she cannot have our good Mr. Perry to attend her.

No, Mr. Woodhouse is not an old misery, and it is not tedious to go to Hartfield. In fact it is a great pleasure. Mr. Woodhouse is universally beloved for his warm heart and hospitable nature. He cares very much about his friends' health. One must respect the cause though deploring the effect – his often denying his guests the good things provided at his table. His devotion to his daughters, his home, and everyone he is used to is the reason he is no friend to matrimony. Even after seven years and the arrival of the five grandchildren who went to South End, he is still not reconciled to his own daughter's marriage. She, too, is "poor" Isabella.

Well, well, the little peculiarities of one's neighbours do add relish to one's existence, as I must suppose one's own do for them. How different are our lives, my dear Charlotte. Mine, too busy; yours, I suspect, not busy enough.

The commencement of the Michaelmas term is always an anxious time here, especially with new girls to be made comfortable. One such is a little Sukey, aged seven, very homesick and needing much care at present. Her dear mother died, and a desperate father sent her to me. Poor little soul. When she is not at her lessons with the others, I try to keep her by me as much as possible, and when I cannot my good maid Alice, who is quite my right hand in running the school, ties her to her apron strings. I do not think my teachers approve. But in this way the child is never left alone, and she begins to look less unhappy.

I have mentioned to you before one of my older girls, a Harriet Smith, who has been with me since she was was Sukey's age. Now, at seventeen, she is growing into interest and beauty and is almost a woman. I am very fond of her. She is remarkably pretty, with blue eyes and light hair, and a most accommodating disposition. Recently she has been promoted to parlour boarder, which means I see a great deal more of her. I have two of these, the other being a Miss Bickerton.

Harriet is the natural daughter of a decent and prosperous tradesman who supports her in a most liberal manner, but wishes for anonymity. Indeed, I have told her nothing, and fortunately she displays very little curiosity as to her parentage: the school having been her only home for almost as long as she can remember.

I do not know what will become of her. She is not accomplished enough to seek a post as governess, and has no dowry to tempt a man of property. I do have private hopes, however, of one Robert Martin, brother of two girls who were here at school, and with whom Harriet spent most of this summer past. He is a good, steady young man and very kind to his widowed mother and sisters. The family rents a farm of Mr. Knightley at Donwell. I believe Mr. Knightley thinks most highly of them.

I hope all this inconsequential chatter does not bore you to death – as you used to say. Are you really beginning to take more interest in the affairs of Highbury? Certainly I cannot run on in this gossipy manner to anyone else. It would be most unseemly and indecorous in "Mrs. Goddard, the mistress of the school".

Well, well, I must go now and give encouragement in the kitchen where they are baking the apple tarts which the children so much enjoy – indeed, many of the older ones have helped to pick the fruit off our own trees in the garden.

The name of Mr. Weston's son is Frank Churchill of Enscombe. Presumably his aunt and uncle required this of him. He has not yet paid his expected visit, by the way. I hope for Mrs. Weston's sake that he does not put it off too much longer.

Now please let me hear that you are following my advice.

I remain with love,
Yrs affectionately,
M. Goddard.

LETTER 6

From Mrs. Pinkney to Mrs. Goddard

Sloane Street,
London
21 October 1813

My dear Mary,

Apple tarts! Bless me! I am persuaded the poor young ladies at the seminary next door would be in a positive ecstasy if they could but taste of such a treat. How can I possibly know such a thing? Read on, and you shall hear.

But before I embark on the history of that little adventure, I admit, though it costs me a pang to do so, that your rebuke is justified. The present state of affairs, I will acknowledge I brought entirely upon myself, and no doubt I have got my just deserts.

Had Mr. Grenville left me with even a tolerable maintenance, I would never have considered Mr. P.'s offer, but I was desirous of a comfortable provision, and thus have I been served. Provision I have, but Mr. P.'s reserved and silent temper and his gout, which came upon him only since we have been married, take most of the comfort away.

But you do not want to hear about grievances, but about apple tarts.

Yesterday Betty was polishing the front door knocker when a group of the girls passed by returning to dinner from their walk. Imagine her consternation when one of them faltered, took hold of our railing, and collapsed right on our very steps. There was a grand to-do. Hysterics and noise which brought me down from my window in the drawing room. The teacher accompanying them, a young woman not much older than her charges, stood wringing her hands helplessly while the girls milled about buzzing like bees, and Betty, sensible person that she is, was doing what she could, supporting the head of the young lady, and patting her face, trying to bring her round. This was the scene when I arrived. I soon applied the lavender drops I had snatched up from my bureau, and gradually the young lady regained consciousness.

I was able to persuade the dithering teacher to remove her swarm of pupils, and told her that when the poor fainting one had sufficiently recovered I would send her back to the school with Betty.

We helped Miss Gordon, for that was her name, into the dining room and gave her some brandy and water. She seemed to be about seventeen years of age, and not nearly as fashionable or well-dressed as the other girls I have observed. She was a little timid and reluctant to volunteer, but in due course it all came out. She had had a slight indisposition that morning and been late rising. The housekeeper or the mistress, I am not sure which, had denied her any breakfast. When she fainted on our doorstep, it was three o'clock in the afternoon and she had not eaten since the previous day.

This we remedied at once, you may be sure. Cold meats and cheese and fruit were brought in, and even the remains of an apple tart! After very little persuasion she made a most tolerable meal. But I was so provoked by the circumstance that when she was ready to leave I determined myself to escort her back to the school; I would speak to Madame Dubois and give her a piece of my mind.

But such was not to be. The supercilious manservant who opened the door – yes, Mary, an indoor manservant in a girls' school, it shows you the pretentions of the place – had obviously been apprised of the mishap. In an insolent manner he declared that if I wished to see Madame I could not. She was not at home. "Indeed?" said I, almost certain he was lying. He smirked knowingly and with false ceremony inquired whether I wished to leave a message. "Yes. Mrs. Pinkney's compliments and she recommends that Madame Dubois try feeding her pupils for a change."

No doubt highly improper. But I was so angry I could not

help myself. The man gave an explosive snigger, and even Miss Gordon attempted to conceal a smile. I was glad to have amused her, for I had little hope of the servant reporting what I had said. It would not be becoming in him to repeat a criticism of the food, and I have no doubt he sees to it that *he* always gets enough to eat! Ten minutes later, back at home and looking out from my window, I saw with my own eyes Madame Dubois leave the house. "Not at home", she may have been, but "out" she certainly was not.

I had parted from Miss Gordon with instructions to come and see me again whenever she felt inclined. I hope she does. She seems a pretty-spoken young lady, though not in good spirits. She has the most amazing red hair, large sad grey eyes and freckles. Yes, dear Mary, I can read your thoughts; taking an interest in this waif will give me an occupation, something else to think about besides myself.

I know you have advised me to make the best of my marriage to Mr. P., but I am entirely convinced that his coming into Yorkshire as an old friend of Mr. Grenville to attend the funeral, and his subsequent protestations of regard, were but a device to procure for himself a housekeeper at the minimum of expense. That his housekeeper of twenty-five years (for Mr. P. had his own establishment at Cambridge) had left him only shortly before our marriage to live with a widowed sister, does, you must admit, lend credence to this view.

There is further proof in the fact that when we were married he positively refused to buy a carriage. In thus completely flouting the usual convention, he has further reduced me to the level of housekeeper. He declares that there is no call for a carriage, in London, where there are plenty of Hackney coaches to be had, and since we never go visiting, there is no occasion for the expenditure. How very different from Mr. Grenville. *There* expense was never a consideration.

Nevertheless, I shall pay heed to your advice and attempt a reformation. Heaven knows there is nothing to be lost, though heaven knows, also, what can be gained? I admit I should not have spoken of him thus. His ankle is much swollen and he is in great pain. The disease comes and goes, it seems. I think I told you there was no sign of it when we were first married. Mr. Wingfield came again yesterday and drew off eight ounces of blood. He stopped to chat with me for a few minutes before leaving. I was not able to find out anything of interest about the John Knightleys. You do not begrude me this little harmless curiosity, do you? A civil inquiry as to the health of the family in Brunswick Square brought only the information that the baby was teething.

So Frank Weston is Frank Churchill. No, I do not *know* the young gentleman, but I have always known *of* him, without realizing that he was the son of your "general favourite", Mr. Weston. Our vicar, when I lived in Yorkshire, a very scholarly gentleman, and friend of Mr. Grenville, used to ride ten miles three times a week to tutor the young Churchill in Greek and Latin. He often spoke of Enscombe and this little boy, and of course I remember the circumstance as being somewhat unusual. A very bright and lively lad, he said, taken from his widowed father and adopted by the Churchills. Dr. Evans was not one to speak ill of others, but I particularly remember his saying – and this must be nearly fifteen years ago – that Mrs. Churchill was a very capricious woman with the devil of a temper and though she doted on the child, she was often out of humour, and any consistency of behaviour towards either the boy or her husband could never be depended upon.

Mr. Churchill, apparently, is a very decent sort of fellow, but completely governed by his wife, which is all the more strange because the money is his, and she was nobody of any consequence before her marriage. But why am I telling you this? It can never affect you at Highbury.

And speaking of such things: Lord, Mary, I hope you may soon get your parlour boarders off your hands. They are young now. But supposing they do not marry? A shocking prospect to have two old spinsters living with you forever. How *I* should dislike having to share my parlour and my dining table with others. But then I have been ever a selfish creature, which *you* are not!

Adieu,

Charlotte

LETTER 7

From Mrs. Goddard to Mrs. Pinkney

Highbury,
28 October 1813

My dear Charlotte,

You will not like what I am about to say. I am sorry, but I simply cannot believe that Mr. Pinkney married you merely to gain a housekeeper. Also I regret that I cannot be sympathetic in the matter of your not having a carriage. On the contrary, it appears to me to be a most sensible measure. Surely after your experience with Mr. Grenville you should welcome some restraint and moderation when it comes to spending money.

Before you become angry with me, I will hasten to say that with the rest of your letter I am entirely prepared to sympathize.

I was exceedingly distressed to hear of that poor young lady fainting from hunger. Can Madame Dubois be aware? I know she runs a fashionable seminary, and her ideas and her school are very different from mine, but surely she would not accept money for board, and then withold that board? It must be some dishonest housekeeper who has her own profit in view? I hope you are able to investigate the matter and do something for poor Miss Gordon.

As for Madame instructing the servant to say she was not at home, of course I do not approve, and would never, I hope, do such a thing myself, but I understand that it is the custom in London, in smart society, to deny a person one does not wish to see. Who knows what cares may have been occupying her at the very moment you called? The mistress of a school has much to contend with.

As you may judge, I speak with feeling. This morning the old writing master burst in upon me in a perfect fury. The spare bottle of ink he could swear was on the shelf had disappeared. "Stolen" he declared. I am to order more at once from London, and this time I am to make certain that is is not so pale as the last lot! Having delivered himself of this diatribe, he whirled out of my room again without so much as a "Good Morning." He is an excellent instructor, so I must put up with his tantrums and eccentricities.

On a happier note, I am pleased to report that I have been able to bring off a little coup I have long had in contemplation. I was spurred on by the recent return of Harriet Smith from the long visit to the Martins, the friends I told you of. She has been rather low-spirited. Quite understandably it is difficult for her to settle back into the routine of the school in which she has lived so long after the more carefree pleasures and evening games at Abbey-Mill Farm.

So when Miss Woodhouse invited the good Bateses and myself – as she often does – to play cards with her father at Hartfield, I took up my pen and requested that I might bring Miss Smith with me. A most civil and obliging invitation was returned.

Harriet has often admired Miss Woodhouse at a distance – in church and in the High Street, and the prospect of such an evening was delightful to her. At the same time she was quite in awe of the invitation: Hartfield, of whose elegance she had often heard – being, along with Donwell Abbey, the first house in consequence here.

Of course she was anxious to make a favourable impression. She begged the two Abbots and myself to come into her room to inspect her wardrobe. After much going through the contents of her closet, the choice came down to a white spotted muslin or a pale blue sarsenet. I let the girls give their opinion first, and luckily we all agreed that although the blue sarsnet matched her eyes, the spotted muslin was more elegant for Hartfield.

Mr. Woodhouse always sends his carriage for us on these occasions. James arrived most punctually at the school: we then collected Mrs. and Miss Bates from their house in the High

Street. They were ready for us at the bottom of their stairs. The horses must not be kept waiting!

I am happy to say my little *protégée*, although quite in a flutter of spirits, behaved herself admirably. She has not a great understanding, but is natural and unaffected with very pleasing manners. These attributes, and her own beauty, make her an agreeable ornament in any drawing-room. I believe I may give myself some credit in as much as I have had the entire bringing-up of her since she was a child of seven years old.

While we four older people played piquet, I observed that Miss Woodhouse was talking to Harriet very graciously. The supper was most delectable, as it always is at Hartfield – chicken and scalloped oysters. On its arrival, the usual contest took place: Miss Woodhouse attempting to do the honours of the meal and fill the plates and glasses of her guests, while her father endeavoured to prevent us enjoying the good things out of concern for our health. Poor Mrs. Bates, who does dearly love her food, hardly knew how to resist the boiled egg Mr. Woodhouse was pressing upon her. He kept assuring her that an egg boiled very soft was not unwholesome and that Serle understood the boiling of an egg better than anybody. The expression on the good old lady's face, torn as she was between civility and appetite, was quite comical to behold.

Harriet was most impressed by everything in such a luxurious style and was quite overcome, when we left, by Miss Woodhouse actually shaking her hand! So you can see that it was a most gratifying and successful evening.

I believe the friendship bids fair to flourish, and it will do very well to fill in the time before Robert Martin makes his offer, because make it, I am convinced he will.

I do not believe I mentioned that when Harriet returned from Abbey-Mill Farm, Mrs. Martin sent with her a very fine goose? So very kind, and so very much appreciated. We ate it for our Michaelmas dinner. I invited the three teachers, Miss Nash, Miss Prince and Miss Richardson to dine with the two parlour boarders and me, and very much did we enjoy ourselves. We had, as well, some boiled trout, a *ragoût* and several side dishes followed by a whipt syllabub. Not the usual school fare, I can assure you.

Really, dear Charlotte, how can you possibly talk of two girls of seventeen and eighteen becoming "old spinsters"? I have every expectation that Harriet will soon be the wife of Robert Martin, and undoubtedly Miss Bickerton, although rather a dull young woman, will succeed in finding *someone* to marry.

In reprobating my having parlour boarders, you forget that I have my way to make in the world. All the regular school fees I receive are used to improve the premises, pay the teachers and servants and supply good food. I have my old age to consider. Income from the parlour boarders goes into a little nest egg. A small cottage somewhere in the environs of Highbury, along the Donwell road, is what I have in mind.

I hope Mr. Pinkney's gout improves and that you have seen the young lady again.

Yours aff:ly,

M. Goddard

P.S. What you have to tell me about the Churchills explains Mr. Weston's reluctance to talk much about them. He is always very guarded in his references, though he has dropped hints that *she* is not the most agreeable woman in the world.

LETTER 8

From Mrs. Pinkney to Mrs. Goddard

Sloane Street,
31 October 1813

My dear Mary,

I have just this moment closed the door upon Charlotte Gordon. She called this morning to thank me for my assistance, and would have come sooner, I gather, but could not obtain permission to leave the premises from the wretched Madame Dubois.

Yes, wretched she is, indeed. I know you are reluctant to think ill of anybody. But I assure you, you may think as ill as you please of her, and it will never be ill enough.

I took the child upstairs to the parlour, put forward my best efforts to make her feel at home. It was pouring with rain outside, but she arrived with no umbrella, wearing a very thin and shabby pelisse and worn shoes, which were quite soaked through: even though she had only come from next door. She was absolutely shivering with cold. I made up the fire, placed a chair beside it, and begged her to warm herself. She told me she is never really warm in winter. But then she is so thin, and Madame Dubois apparently does not permit more than the feeblest flicker of flame in any of the grates at the school. So the heat is evidently on a par with the food. I rang for refreshments, muffin and hot chocolate, and, once she had overcome her civil scruples, it was astonishing to see how much the poor child was able to consume!

I do feel for this young lady. So pale. So white. So melancholy. And then having the same name as myself. Another Charlotte! *There* is an additional charm! She has evidently a very low opinion of herself. I gathered she considers she is very plain, owing to her red hair. But I am persuaded that if she were properly fed and in better spirits, she might be nearer to being pretty, in an uncommon way.

I do not know what it is that troubles her, but I shall find out in due course, you may be sure. She says she has no friends among the older girls, not being as well-dressed as they or having pocket money with which to buy bonbons and treats. She finds her amusement in reading aloud to the younger ones. They huddle in some room in the attic where they are undisturbed, though freezing cold. Just now they are embarked on *The Governess*. She says they all wish that they had a charming arbour in which to talk privately like the pupils at Mrs. Teachum's academy, where it seems to be always summer!

She was amused when I told her how you and I used to laugh

together over that book when we were girls; how we thought that no set of human beings could be so perfect as Miss Fielding had portrayed them. I sometimes wonder if you took the idea for your own school from *The Governess*? It is, to be sure, very much more like Mrs. Teachum's academy than is that horrid seminary next door.

I have invited Charlotte to call whenever she is able. I rather regret my hasty and ill-considered remark to the servant (which I *now* trust was not repeated!) I have sent a polite note to Madame Dubois to ease the way for Charlotte's visits, though I can tell you it cost me dear to pen the conciliating words. Mr. P., who has not yet met Charlotte, being closeted in his room both times she was here, I have advised of the circumstance, and he says he has no objection to the acquaintance if it affords me any amusement.

So you did not scruple to beg for an invitation for Harriet to Hartfield? Was it wise, dear Mary? This elegant Miss Woodhouse, whose abode is first in consequence in Highbury, is she a fit companion do you think for your little rustic bastard?

Ever yours,
Charlotte

LETTER 9

From Mrs. Goddard to Mrs. Pinkney

Highbury,
16 November 1813

I am very much displeased, which is why I have not written. Really Charlotte, I must take you to task for such language.

Everyone knows there are many ways of describing the same object according to the perspective of the viewer. In strict legal truth Harriet is, I suppose, "a bastard," but that does not alter the fact that she is a most beautiful young woman with modest and engaging manners.

I am excessively glad that Miss Woodhouse cannot read what you have written, since words do have power to influence one's ideas. There is no doubt that she believes Harriet to be a gentleman's daughter, and far be it from me to gainsay that impression.

Already, in the short time since that first evening at Hartfield, the friendship blooms, as I firmly believe to the advantage of both young ladies: Harriet is out of the house more frequently, is walking and reading more, and has been cured of her schoolgirl giggle. Miss Woodhouse, having lost her constant companion in marriage to Mr. Weston, I conclude is as delighted with Harriet as Harriet is with her. Furthermore, Harriet tells me that Miss Woodhouse is taking her likeness in water colours.

All the girls in the school are extremely envious, because, to while away any tedium while one young lady is painting, and the other young lady is having to sit still, none other than the great Mr. Elton, himself, has been invited to read aloud to them. So Harriet has the inestimable pleasure of seeing this paragon every day. Not only the girls, but I believe even the teachers would give their all to be in her shoes. Such is the power of the handsome Mr. Elton! If the picture is successful, by the way, it is to be framed and hung in the drawing room at Hartfield.

Does this answer your enquiry as to whether Harriet Smith is a fit companion for Emma Woodhouse?

This is a short letter; but I am out of countenance and can write no more.

Yrs.,

M. Goddard

LETTER 10

From Mrs. Pinkney to Mrs. Goddard

Sloane Street,
London
18 November 1813

I was so glad, my dearest Mary, to hear from you at last. I knew when you did not write that I had offended you, and I do beg your forgiveness for my hasty words. Believe me, I would not hurt your feelings for the world, and if I had thought twice (which I never do!) I should never have spoken thus, knowing how much your pretty little Harriet Smith means to you. You know my tongue was ever too quick, I really have only goodwill in my heart towards your little girl. My excuse must be that my disposition has not been improved by living with one who is so silent and unsociable.

Before your sympathies go all to Mr. P., I must say in my own justification that I did not marry him under any false pretence. You know how dearly I loved Mr. Grenville, and I had not completed my year of mourning, but I was so frankly in need of funds, that in every meaning of the word, I could not *afford* to wait so long. Mr. Pinkney was perfectly aware of this. When he made me the offer, I informed him at the time that although I respected him, I could not feel a more tender sentiment, but if he was willing to have me under the circumstances, I would consent to be his wife. He replied in an off-hand manner that he hoped in due course I would feel differently. I assumed that this was said as a matter of form. We agreed on separate bedrooms, and so the bargain was struck. I acquired a maintenance and a home in London, and he, a housekeeper.

On *that* score I think he can have no complaint. It is a matter of honour to me that since he furnishes the roof over my head, I perform my task as well as possible. I see that the house is kept well-ordered and clean and I provide very good dinners, of which he used to eat most heartily, before his present affliction. In fact he has remarked that the food is much better than when Mrs. Wilson was in charge! Once a week he goes through the household accounts – something, needless to say, that Mr. Grenville never did. I will say on Mr. P.'s behalf, however, that he does not begrudge the money, only wants to know how it was spent. I realize *now* that I was a fool to count on any felicity in marriage to a man ten years my senior who has always lived alone.

Oh yes. I know Mr. Grenville was eight years older than me; but *he* married at a reasonable age: Mr. Pinkney did not.

This morning he came into the drawing-room, where I was sitting as usual in the window seat with my book.

"What is that you are reading, Mrs. Pinkney?" said he.

"It is *Evelina*," said I.

"Oh, only a novel" said he. "Some nonsense about a young lady's search for a husband, I suppose."

"And pray, sir," I cried, "what can be more important than a decision on which the whole future of a woman's happiness depends?"

To my mortification, the tears commenced to roll down my cheeks. Me, at my age! Still I do very much feel that in marrying Mr. P. I have given up all hope of ever being happy again. He was quite at a loss, would fear that I was ill, and would ring the bell for Betty. Having nothing whatever to say in extenuation, I got up and left the room, retiring to my chamber where I knew he would not follow me.

Ah, my dear Mary, with what pain do I recollect the carefree past. What charming memories I have of our childhood together in my father's parsonage.

Such companions we were, despite the difference in our ages. Remember the day I ran out of the garden to join the village children picking blackberries in the hedgerow? I was six, I believe, and you were eleven. You tried to make me return, and when you could not, you came along, for you would not let me out of your sight. I covered my clothes with blackberry juice. Do you remember? How vexed our poor mother was! Then there was that hot day when I insisted we paddle in Farmer Holt's stream. Nobody would ever have found out if that naughty Tom had not come along and hidden our shoes and stockings. I was ever getting us into mischief, and always against your advice and better judgement. Poor Mary, how good you were. And what you had to put up with. Ah, but those were delightful times. When one has kind parents and a happy home, it leads one to expect much happiness in life thereafter. Well, at least we both *began* our adult life that way even if it has not continued to be so.

All this was brought to mind this evening. At dinner, Mr. P., after the *contretemps* of the morning, treated me with the greatest consideration and was actually disposed to conversation. He inquired after you! He has never evinced the smallest interest before. He observed that judging by the frequency of our correspondence, we must be very fond of one another. I said we were. That I would rather spend such shillings as I had on letters from you than on any other object. He inquired what manner of woman you were. Were we alike? I said, indeed we were not in the least alike. That you were a kind, motherly person of the highest principles, who some seventeen years ago, had lost all your sweet babes in one week to the scarlet fever. Mr. P. made very proper expressions of sympathy and horror. Then I told him how shortly thereafter Mr. Goddard, too, had succumbed, and that I had gone from Yorkshire to be with you in your affliction.

"It must have been great, indeed, madam," he said.

"It was, sir," said I, "but never shall I forget my sister's fortitude. Gradually her religious mind and cheerful disposition led her to acceptance." After a suitable moment of silence, Mr. P. was disposed to wonder why you had not married again.

"Marry again!" cried I, overcome with the remembrance of lost happiness. "My sister's love for Mr. Goddard, and his for her, was such as could never be replaced."

"That I can well understand, madam," said he with a slight bow.

I recollected myself. He was referring, no doubt, to my previous happy marriage to his friend Mr. Grenville, and contrasting it with our own sad and joyless union. I continued more calmly, thinking I would turn the conversation into less dangerous channels.

"Mrs. Goddard's life is very full," I said. "Mr. Goddard left her with a small competence, and since she was always fond of young people she removed to Highbury, in a healthy part of Surry, and became the mistress of a school."

"She was very courageous, madam."

"Yes," said I, by now determined to give him the full history. "She found a house with an ample garden and caused a sign to be erected at the gate. I remember her telling me exactly how it read, for she had considered the matter most carefully: 'Mrs. Goddard's School. Young Ladies Boarded. Moderate Terms. Dancing, Writing, Musick, French and all Female Accomplishments.'"

Are you not impressed by my memory, dear Mary? For of course I have never seen this sign. I imagine it in white paint on a green board. Am I correct?

Mr. P. appeared to be interested, and so I continued. "At first she had only six pupils and one maidservant, but she attracted the notice of a Mr. Woodhouse, chief gentleman of the place. He advised and encouraged her in many little matters, and observing that the children flourished under her care, recommended her among his acquaintance. In due time she was able to acquire the neighboring property. Now she has over forty young ladies in her school, and I believe a waiting list besides."

"Most exemplary," said Mr. Pinkney, "Mrs. Goddard must indeed be a most admirable person."

"She is," said I. Dear Mary, I am ashamed to tell you, but again a tear rolled down my cheek. I never was one for crying before! "She is the most admirable person I have ever known," I said. Then gathering my courage together, I continued, "I have not met her since that great tragedy seventeen years ago. I should so much like to see her again."

"You have mentioned this before," said he. "At present it is not at all convenient." And he went on to aver that he could not spare me just now with his gout so bad, and after all we had only been married three months, and people would think it very odd if I left him to go visiting. I forebore to inquire what people he was referring to, since he was either out at his club, or shut up in his study with his books and his chess game twelve hours of the twenty-four. Still, despite this little impediment – and after all I had not really expected him to acquiesce – the evening passed a great deal more pleasantly than usual.

Am I forgiven?

Yrs. affectionately,

Charlotte

LETTER 11

From Mrs. Goddard to Mrs. Pinkney

The School,

Highbury,

22 November 1813

My dear Charlotte,

Of course you are forgiven. Let us not mention the subject again.

From what you say, it seems to me that Mr. Pinkney is a somewhat sad and lonely figure, and perhaps more sensitive than you give him credit for? Be kind to him, my dear. As Mr. Grenville's closest friend he must have some good qualities.

So you were able to say something of our youth and family? Strange that he never wanted to hear, or you to tell him before. How vividly your recollections called to mind the dear old days at the rectory. But your praise of me is quite undeserved. I have my faults like everyone else, one of which is to lecture like a schoolmarm. And there is no particular merit in doing well what one enjoys. I have always loved young people and the interest in seeing them grow and develop. Like Thomson, I find it,

> Delightful task! To rear the tender thought,
> To teach the young idea how to shoot.

Actually, young Sukey is playing with her doll at my feet as I write. She is singing to herself and talking to the doll, which pleases me very much.

In contrast to your seminary next door, I do not aim to bring up prodigies, but only amiable young women who will become good wives and mothers, or at least be a credit and a comfort to their near relations.

That being said, I must go and attend to those same young ladies. It is my evening for reading and sewing together with the older ones. By a strange coincidence our present book is *Evelina!* I make the girls take it in turns to read aloud. Even Shakespeare knew the advantage of a modulated voice and proper intonation in a woman. We sit in my parlour with a good fire, and I believe the girls look forward to this weekly event very much indeed.

Yours aff.,

M. Goddard

P.S. Yes, you are pretty correct about the sign. Your inquiry reminds me that it is in need of re-painting, and a branch has grown across. I must get John to see to it.

LETTER 12

From Mrs. Pinkney to Mrs. Goddard

Sloane Street,
London
28 November 1813

What a pretty picture you paint, my dear Mary. The difference between your school and the life there, and that of the girls next door, here, is deplorable indeed.

The more you tell me, the more I wish I could see it. Fancy your reading *Evelina*! I am got almost to the end of it, but have not had so much time for reading as before.

I am happy to report that Mr. P.'s gout is a little better. Mr. Wingfield has been almost every day to see him and is pleased with his progress. My inquiries about the family in Brunswick Square have now reached that degree of intimacy that he actually informed me that they (the John Knightleys) are to go to Highbury for Christmas. That seemed to be the cue for me to tell him that I had a sister living there. He asked me if I knew the John Knightleys, and I said I did not. But your letters, dear Mary, are making me so familiar with the good souls in Highbury that I almost feel I would recognize them if I were to meet them on the street. Though when that day may be, who can say?

Charlotte Gordon now visits quite frequently and Mr. P. has met her at last. He came unexpectedly into the parlour a few days ago while we were sitting together. The poor man looked quite frightened. For a moment I thought he might run away. He is not used to young ladies and I believe knows not how to address one.

Charlotte has told me that she is an orphan, and that her fees, greatly reduced from the usual charge, are paid by a great aunt, who is an old friend of Madame Dubois. I encouraged her to say more, but she is reserved, and does not talk about herself, I believe from a fear of being hurt rather than a wish to be secretive. So we speak mostly about the school – the dancing master has just run off with the Italian mistress – and the strange fads and foibles of Madame Dubois whose chief interest lies in the dissipated social life she leads in the evenings. The school can go hang, as far as I can gather!

Well, I am sure you will want to know how Charlotte is as to *health*. You can be certain that I always see that she has chocolate and a muffin or cold meat or anything else she may fancy whenever she comes over here. If I can prevail, I give her some food to carry away. I am pleased that she seems to enjoy my company. At least mine is a sympathetic ear, but I must not flatter myself. I expect it is only the muffin she comes for.

Yesterday, Mr. P., to my surprise, came and joined us in the parlour. After a time, he began to talk to Charlotte of books. Upon her admitting that she reads aloud to the younger ones, he mentioned that his eyes often grow tired, especially in the winter when the light is poor. She at once said she should be happy to oblige, only she did not know if her performance would be satisfactory given the sort of works she presumed he preferred. Mr. P. made a suitable rejoinder and then, emboldened perhaps by her complaisance, he inquired from whom had she inherited her red hair?

To my astonishment, this innocent question quite upset the girl, her face grew pink and she looked as if she would burst into tears. I hastily intervened and saved her from the necessity of a reply by asking her if she would ring the bell for more hot water. Mr. P., quite flustered by this disconcerting response to his conversational gambit, fell silent. Why should she be so distressed? Can she be someone's natural daughter, another bastard, do you suppose?

Which brings me to your own Harriet Smith and her friend; I am glad if you feel the intimacy prospers to their mutual advantage. When I suggested that they were not fit companions for each other, I thought not of Miss Woodhouse, but of the evil that might be done to Harriet in becoming accustomed to more

43

elegant surroundings than she will have whenever she marries this Robert Martin you are so certain of.

Your aff. sister,
Charlotte

LETTER 13

From Mrs. Goddard to Mrs. Pinkney

Highbury
5 December 1813

My dear Charlotte,

I am delighted you are receiving pleasure from the companionship of your young namesake. Friendship with a young person does keep one more active both in body and mind than one otherwise might be. I think I may say from my own experience that no amount of muffin would entice her to your fireside, did she not find your company congenial. As for her red hair, it is possible, being the age that she is, that the colour vexes her so much she cannot bear to speak of it or have it mentioned.

What you tell me of the seminary of Madame Dubois is truly lamentable. She appears to be a thoroughly wicked woman. I have heard of such places, where vanity and accomplishments are considered more important than health and kindness. Thank goodness I have never had personal experience of any such evil.

Meanwhile, and talking of young people, I have some excellent news to report from here. I have reason to believe that what I have been hoping and praying for has happened; I speak, of course, of Robert Martin's proposal of marriage to Harriet Smith.

An hour ago the young man called. I was passing through the hall when he rang the bell, and was behind Alice when she opened the door. He called out to me, "Good morning, Mrs. Goddard," and walking directly by Alice he held out a small parcel with both hands. "This is from my sister," said he, giving it into my care as if it were the crown jewels, "Would you be so kind as to see that it is safely delivered to Miss Smith?"

"Yes, indeed," said I, amused at his emphasis on the *safely delivered*, "but would you not rather wait and give it to her yourself? She will be back very shortly, I believe."

"Oh, no," he said, turning quite scarlet, "that would not do at all." And observing my look of astonishment, he hastily declared that he was obliged to return to the farm, for he had an appointment with Mr. Knightley and William Larkins about his sheep.

So off he went, and when Harriet returned, (she had been at Hartfield since breakfast) I gave her the parcel myself, mentioning that Robert Martin had brought it. She took it with a blush of surprise, and ran away to the parlour, where I, happening to come in some minutes later to collect the account book from my desk, found her sitting, eagerly perusing a letter, with music scattered about on the floor that in her haste had evidently fallen there. She gave a little start when I entered, hastily collected up the papers, remarking that it was songs Elizabeth was returning and said that she must leave at once to see Miss Woodhouse.

"But you have just come from Hartfield?" said I. She said yes, to be sure, but she was going back there directly for dinner and she had something very particular to tell Miss Woodhouse that would admit of no delay, and away she ran, hardly stopping to put on her bonnet and shawl.

I was frankly disappointed she did not take me into her confidence, but I suppose it is only natural in the circumstances that she should wish that her intimate friend should be the first to share her good fortune. I have not the slightest doubt that the letter was from Robert Martin. No communication from his sister would provoke so much perturbation. I tell you frankly, Charlotte, this is quite the realization of my fondest hopes for the child. No marriage could be more eligible or more conducive to her happiness than with this most estimable young man. As they have nothing to wait for, I hope to see her installed at the Abbey Mill Farm within the next few months, and I only await confirmation from her own lips before I write to her father. How pleased the good man will be. I know her future has been of concern to him.

Alice has just come in. Little Sukey has a sore throat and a fever, and she thinks we should send for Mr. Perry at once. I am quite alarmed.

Next Day. I have not had time to take up my pen again until now. I was afraid the child might have some serious malady, a dread which is always with me since the loss of my own dear ones; but Mr. Perry assures us it is only a bad cold.

Well, one worry soon supplants another, especially when there are so many young people under one's care. Harriet has just walked in from Hartfield where she spent the night. I was very pleased to see her, and expected her momentarily to announce her engagement. But no. To my surprise she is in very low spirits, and ill-disposed to conversation. What can this mean? She says only that she has come to collect her things, for she has been invited to spend several days with Miss Woodhouse.

I could have sworn from everything I observed that Mr. Martin had made her an offer: his manner when he delivered the letter, her eagerness while she read it, her rush to be off to Hartfield, all bespoke a more than ordinary communication.

I am aware that Miss Woodhouse considers the Martins as beneath her notice. But that should not affect Harriet whom I have been at particular pains to breed up (because of her parentage) to be a modest girl without undue expectations.

Surely Miss Woodhouse's low opinion of the Martin family could not carry any weight with her? She, whose best friend Elizabeth Martin has ever been while she was at the school; to say nothing of the long sojourn she spent this summer at Abbey-Mill Farm? Is it possible that the affection and friendship of years could be put in the balance of Miss Woodhouse's disapprobation and found wanting?

I did ask Harriet if anything was amiss. She said no, nothing, while her looks spoke exactly the reverse. Delicacy forbade further inquiry. But if she does not marry Robert Martin, whom else can she marry? Heaven forbid that she should be reduced to the old writing master's son!

It seems beyond belief that Emma Woodhouse could actually have persuaded Harriet to refuse him. Such a worthy, decent young man, whose name has seldom been off her lips for the past two months.

I sadly fear that you were only too correct in your conjecture that no good would come of this intimacy between the two girls. Dear Charlotte, I begin to rue the day I ever introduced the one to the other.

Pray excuse me if I pour onto you all my little anxieties and cares. I have no one else in whom I can confide. The mistress of a school is like the captain of a ship, alone responsible for the welfare, guidance, life, and safety of all who sail in her.

Your troubled sister,
Mary Goddard

LETTER 14

From Mrs. Pinkney to Mrs. Goddard

Sloane Street,
London
10 December 1813

My dear Mary,

I am exceedingly sorry to hear what you say of your Harriet. It does appear quite evident to me that her friend has persuaded her against accepting Robert Martin. But then someone like Emma Woodhouse, handsome, clever and rich, as you describe her, would not look kindly upon a young farmer as the prospective husband of her bosom friend – especially since she does not appear to have a young man in view for herself?

I know how much you had set your heart on this match, and I grieve for your distress. How foolish of Harriet to turn down such an unexceptionable offer.

If you are saddened by the behaviour of *your* young lady, I must report that our lives have been considerably brightened by what I may call *ours*. As you suggested, seldom as either Mr. P. or I have ever been friendly with a young person, we find it a most refreshing novelty. We are, besides, quite taken with this particular young lady with her flaming red hair and large, sad eyes.

Her eyes may be sad, but they are young and strong. At Mr. P.'s request, she has been reading aloud to us – Shakespeare or the Spectator or Dr. Johnson. She has a charming voice and a quick understanding. So he sits with his leg upon a footstool and I listen and make a pretence of doing my tapestry work, amazed to find myself a part of such a pretty domestic scene. I confess that there is something about hearing these difficult works read aloud which makes them much easier to apprehend. Charlotte told me privately that she enjoyed the stimulus of being required to consider authors that she might not pick up for pleasure merely.

In consequence, I am glad to say that Mr. P. has become more sociable. The horrible yellow Mr. Fowler is in the country and the chess board is put away for the time being. Mr. P. now makes a greater effort to converse at meals. You will not be surprised to hear that our subject is very often Charlotte.

And now, if you please, we are to go to Bath over the Christmas season! Bath, do I hear you say? Five times as far as Highbury. But the decision is not of my making or you know which place I would choose. Mr. P. has arranged to meet a childhood friend of his there, an Admiral Seymour, whom he has not seen for many years. He has high hopes that the waters will prove beneficial to his gout and Mr. Wingfield has been encouraging him in the notion. We are spared sea-bathing, at least.

Yours affectionately,

C. Pinkney

LETTER 15

From Mrs. Goddard to Mrs. Pinkney

Highbury,
16 December 1813

My dear Charlotte,

I am delighted you are finding Mr. P. more conversible. If one cannot talk to one's husband, to whom else can one talk? It also pleases me to think of you in Bath, where I hope you will find some diversion.

You are quite mistaken in your assumption that Miss Woodhouse regrets that she has no young man in view for herself. Harriet tells me that she has vowed she will never marry. Indeed, it is not so very surprising. Mistress of Hartfield, as she is, with everything money can buy or her heart desire, and living with someone who dotes upon her, she could hardly improve upon her *situation*. The usual inducements to seek a husband that animate most young women, are not present in the case of Miss Woodhouse.

Alice was just leaving for the post office when I closed my last to you, or I should have added that a few minutes later made an inexplicable alteration in Harriet. From looking as downcast as possible, she returned to my room to take her leave, a transformed young lady, her face positively wreathed in smiles. I had heard her talking with Miss Nash while she was packing, and on my later inquiring what had transpired to restore Harriet's good-humour – Miss Nash said it was only some trifling gossip Mr. Perry had told her when he came to see Sukey.

As he was coming home from Clayton Park he had encountered Mr. Elton. Mr. Elton was in very good spirits and on his way up to London with a package. Since it was their whist club

49

night, Mr. Perry begged him to postpone the errand until the next day; he being their best player would be very much missed. But Mr. Elton was adamant. He had an "enviable commission" and was the bearer of "something exceedingly precious." From his manner Mr. Perry gathered there was a lady in the case, especially since Mr. Elton had never missed a club night before.

All this Mr. Perry recounted to Miss Nash, and since Mr. Elton's affairs are of absorbing interest to every unmarried female in the place, she repeated it to Harriet, who was extremely diverted, apparently, especially by the "something exceedingly precious". She evidently knew what it was. But why that should effect such a miraculous transformation in her state of mind, I do not begin to comprehend. I hope she is not setting her cap at Mr. Elton, for I am certain she has no chance there. Simple young creature that she is, she is not aware how the misfortune of her birth might deter most men from making her an offer of marriage.

I conclude quite definitely that she has refused Robert Martin. Further proof in the matter is that neither Elizabeth nor her sister have been near the school since he left off the parcel. This is a most unusual circumstance, especially at this Christmas season: the two Martins were in the habit of very frequently calling in to see their old schoolfellows.

My heart aches for the disappointment of the young man, and the feelings of mortification that must be endured by his mother and sisters. After all their kindness and hospitality, how ungrateful they must deem her; not, of course, that that is a reason for accepting an uncongenial proposal; but until she was introduced at Hartfield, Harriet thought the Martins of Abbey Mill Farm quite a nonpareil among families; they and their concerns formed the chief subject of her conversation every hour of every day.

Her latest diversion is the collecting of riddles and charades. It is an occupation she has learned from Miss Nash, who is a great collector of mottoes, having over 300 in one book as well as all the texts from which Mr. Elton ever preached in another. Harriet's collection I have seen, and very well done it is. She writes a pretty hand, if I do say so. But then my old writing master does know his business. One riddle, however, is in Miss Woodhouse's handwriting. It is an elegant charade which, Harriet said with a blush, had been supplied by Mr. Elton. What this signifies, I leave you, dear Charlotte, with your taste for mysteries to decipher. I thought you would be interested to see it, so I asked Hariet if I might borrow her book and then got one of the younger girls who needs practice in writing to copy it out for me. Here it is:

To Miss –
CHARADE
My first displays the wealth and pomp of kings,
Lords of the earth! their luxury and ease.
Another view of man, my second brings,
Behold him there, the monarch of the seas!

But, ah! united, what reverse we have!
Man's boasted power and freedom, all are flown;
Lord of the earth and sea, he bends a slave,
And woman, lovely woman, reigns alone.

Thy ready wit the word will soon supply,
May its approval beam in that soft eye!

Rather clever, do not you think? One is almost surprised that Mr. Elton could have composed it, though at the time, I believe, he did say it was written by a friend.

Surely, however, he cannot be courting *Harriet*? Quite impossible! It must be Miss Woodhouse? All I hope is that this "Courtship" charade, in conjunction with the episode of the journey to London – with whatever it was that was so "exceedingly precious," what extaordinary words to use – do not add encouragement to Harriet's aspirations.

And speaking of Mr. Elton, Harriet told me that she and Miss Woodhouse were actually inside the Vicarage a day or two ago. Apparently Miss Woodhouse's bootlace broke when they were walking in Vicarage Lane, and they were obliged to call upon Mr. Elton's housekeeper to supply a bit of string. Harriet said the prospect from the windows was delightful and the yellow curtains, seen from the road, hang to great advantage in the drawing room. I do not think I have been in that house since old Mr. Bates was vicar. Well, if ever Mr. Elton marries, I presume his lady will entertain again.

Since Harriet is so cheerful and occupied, I suppose, for the moment, I must give over worrying about her future. She is very often at Hartfield, where she has a bedroom appropriated to her own use. Indeed, she spends so much time there that Miss Bickerton, the other parlour boarder, is often at a loss for a companion.

Meantime the rest of the school has benefitted from my *longueurs* over this affair. If ever I am out of sorts I repair to the kitchen and assist with the cooking. That seems to drive all cares from my head. I took little Sukey with me, though Miss Prince did not like that she should miss her spelling lesson. As you may imagine the child greatly enjoyed putting her fingers in the pudding basins and licking them afterwards. Over the last three days we have made Orange Pudding, Two-Penny Pudding and a Spotted Dick. A prodigious quantity of eggs, butter, cream and currants were used – I have, after all, with teachers and servants over fifty people to be fed. Well, it made a festive change to our usual rice puddings and apple dumplings. In this damp, grey weather just before the holidays, the girls were more than ready for a treat. Everything was soon gobbled up.

Yours,

M. Goddard

LETTER 16

From Mrs. Pinkney to Mrs. Goddard

Sloane Street,
18 December 1813

My dear Mary,

Thank you for *Courtship*. "Your ready wit the word will soon supply . . ." Does that sound like Harriet? I have never received the impression from you that she had any wit at all.

All very strange, including the invention of a highly implausible reason to visit the vicarage. At least that is how it appears to me. I suggest that Miss Woodhouse is, indeed, encouraging Harriet to aspire to Mr. Elton.

The invitation to him to read to them every day while the painting was going forward could have many different constructions put upon it. You say Miss W. has sworn she will never marry. But is *Mr. Elton* aware of that fact? As for the thing "exceedingly precious", could it have been the finished painting itself? If it is to hang in the drawing room, presumably it would need to be framed, and that, I suppose, could not be done in Highbury? In conclusion, all I can observe is, that when a handsome, single young man and two pretty young women are thrown together for several hours every day, something is bound to come of it.

Well, from your young lady to mine: at last Charlotte has arrived at a state of mind where she trusts me. Yesterday she told me her story, and knowing it, who can blame her for her melancholy?

A little more than three years ago, her father, Captain Gordon, set sail for the west coast of America, going round the Horn, and has not been heard from since. The Admiralty announced the ship presumed lost with all hands, though no wreckage has ever been found. Shortly after this sad intelligence, the mother, who was consumptive, gave up the ghost and died, but not before writing a letter commending Charlotte to the care of an aunt, the mother's only living relative. This person, a Lady somebody-or-other, was always against her niece's marriage to Captain Gordon, on account of his family not being so great as hers, and from *Scotland* to boot. It appears this aunt has much the same view of the Scotch race as had Dr. Johnson.

Although duty impels her to maintain Charlotte, this aunt actually dislikes and despises the girl, especially on account of her red hair which reminds her of the father from whom she inherited it; such a colour being utterly vulgar and *Scottish* in her opinion. Did you ever hear of anything so unreasonable? This dragon (a fitting friend for Madame Dubois.) lives in Devonshire and comes to London but once a year. So Charlotte has been more or less abandoned at the school. There is talk of her becoming a governess, and when she is eighteen, in a few months time, that is the plan, I believe. The great aunt will then consider her obligation to her dead niece acquitted. Even after all these years, Charlotte clings to the vain hope that her father – whom she worships – is still alive, and that some day or other he will turn up and they will live together happily ever after.

The poor child! She said how much she would miss us over Christmas, and then she went on to reveal that the last two Christmases she has spent almost entirely alone at the seminary with the servants on board wages. While the other young ladies and the teachers have all gone home, the wretched Madame Dubois has gadded about the town leaving Charlotte completely alone and to her own devices.

Hearing this story, and feeling even sorrier for her than usual, last night, with some trepidation, I put the circumstance to Mr. P. To my surprise and delight, he immediately said that it would be an excellent scheme, company for me and a kindness to her, if we were to invite her to join us in Bath. When I think of his refusal to invest in a carriage on our wedding, this offer, so graciously made, was most unexpected, for the extra expense will be considerable.

Luckily Charlotte called today. I at once apprised her of the good news. To my surprise, instead of shouting for joy, she was a little hesitant.

"Oh, madam," said she, "I hope you do not think I was so bold as to be hinting at such a possibility, because, truly, such a thought never entered my head."

"I am sure it did not, my dear. We shall have much pleasure in your company. Accept and think no more of the matter."

She looked me full in the face, then evidently convinced that I meant what I said, she threw her arms round my neck and cried, "Oh, Mrs. Pinkney, what a lucky chance that I should happen to faint upon your doorstep!"

"Dear Charlotte," said I, very touched, "Mr. Pinkney and I are extremely glad if we make you happy."

Charles is gone now to the Golden Cross booking office to engage an extra seat in the coach. I gave him a note to deliver to that miserable woman Madame Dubois requesting permission to take Charlotte with us. I am sure she will make no difficulty. It is one less mouth for her to feed – if you can call it feed. As for the great aunt, she neither knows nor cares what happens to Charlotte.

Address me, when next you write, care of The White Hart, Bath.

Yours in anticipation,
Charlotte

P.S. I shall patronize young Charlotte rather as your Emma Woodhouse does Harriet Smith, but I hope with less harmful consequences. At least I shall not turn aside any young man who might address her, whatever his degree.

LETTER 17

From Mrs. Goddard to Mrs. Pinkney

The School,
Highbury,
21 December 1813

My dear Charlotte,

How very good of Mr. Pinkney to include your young *protégée* in your visit to Bath. I did tell you, did I not, that he would not have been Mr. Grenville's friend for nothing? I hope this arrives in time to welcome you there, and that it finds you safe and well and happily settled into the Inn.

Mr. and Mrs. John Knightley arrived yesterday. This morning Mrs. Knightley came to call on me and brought her five children – Henry, John, George, Bella and little Emma. I was most gratified that she spared the time to come in, since they are here for only one complete week. Mr. John Knightley must be back in town on the 28th. Mrs. Knightley, whom I have known since she was a child, is such a devoted wife and mother, it is quite a joy to see her surrounded by her young family. She is entirely different in temperament and habits from her more brilliant sister. I imagine she takes after her father, and Emma, after her mother.

She did mention their excursion to South End and the benefit they derived from sea-bathing. They had talked about it only the previous evening, apparently, when they were all together with her husband's brother on their first night at Hartfield. Mr. Woodhouse, she said, had been quite distressed that they had not gone to Cromer, which would have been *Mr. Perry's* choice. Mr. Wingfield, however, had recommended South End, and as it was less far to travel, her husband had elected to follow his advice. I judged it better *not* to say Mr. Wingfield was also my sister's husband's apothecary.

From what you tell me, it does appear that your young Charlotte is somewhat in the same case as my Harriet, except that Harriet is surrounded by people who wish her well, and Charlotte seems to have only you and Mr. Pinkney to look out for her.

Meanwhile Christmas rushes towards us, and the weather which was quite mild until only a day or two ago has suddenly changed. We have two or three degrees of frost every night. I ask John to make sure that good fires are kept going but I fear it is not possible to maintain the bedchambers as warm as one would wish. Many of the girls have been suffering dreadfully from chilblains. I dress them with my own hands, because it is not only the medicament, but the sympathy and attention which is most efficacious on these occasions.

I give you my receipt, Charlotte, as I have found it an excellent one. And who knows you may have need of it, for young Charlotte if not for yourself.

CHILBLAIN LINIMENT

Take 1 oz. of camphorated spirits of wine;
½ oz. of Goulard's extract.
Mix and apply 3 or 4 times a day.

Yours affectionately,
M. Goddard

P.S. I shall try and write again before Christmas Day.

57

LETTER 18

From Mrs. Pinkney to Mrs. Goddard

White Hart
Bath
23 December 1813

I am writing this while we wait for breakfast. Really our mails are most expeditious. Your letter was handed to me after we arrived last night. I imagine it had come in the last post, perhaps on the very mail coach on which we were travelling! So if it was *late*, I know the reason why. Oh, my dear Mary, when I think what a tale of tragedy I might have to tell, I feel almost sick with horror.

Meanwhile, here we are safely installed, thank God, with nothing to complain of. Our rooms are very comfortable, and Mr. P.'s friend, Admiral Seymour, has already arrived. My husband is in good spirits at the prospect of some games of chess, and the hope of the waters.

He has been to Bath before, apparently, but for Charlotte and myself, it is all new. As soon as we have had breakfast we mean to walk out and explore. My young friend is most eager to go, in spite of her accident. I would have thought, that under the circumstances, she might have preferred to rest and spend the day quietly. But not a bit of it! The inspiriting glimpses of shops we caught through the coach windows yesterday, as we turned off the London road into Cheap Street, are evidently irresistibly alluring.

Particularly so because my husband has given us yet another proof of whimsical generosity. He economized by travelling on the coach, yet last night night just before retiring, he presented Charlotte with five guineas. "Buy yourself something pretty, my dear," said he, "a Christmas present from an old man, who will have pleasure in seeing you in whatever you choose."

"Oh, sir," she cried, "you are too, too good." And she burst into tears to the consternation of poor Mr. P. The child is so little used to kindness. She has but a very few shillings to her name, and her gowns are in an exceedingly poor way, so five guineas is largesse beyond her wildest dreams.

Later, when I expressed to him my pleasure and gratitude, he said rather unexpectedly that if I was as well pleased as Charlotte, he would be amply repaid. I begin to feel that I may have misjudged him, and to regret my uncharitable remarks. Nevertheless, I still feel constrained in his presence, as if I were but the housekeeper or a visitor under his roof.

So this morning all is anticipation and joy, but, oh, when I think of what might have been! What a narrow escape we had! Instead of laughter and happy plans, I might at this moment be overcome with guilt and grief.

But I must begin at the beginning. Our coach was to depart from the Golden Cross at 5.15 a.m. Charlotte stayed the night with us, and naturally we hardly slept a wink in anticipation of our early start. I had given instructions to the servants that we should be called in good time, but of course had nightmares all night that *they* might oversleep. Nothing untoward of that sort occurred, however. At the appointed hour, Betty brought Charlotte and me a cup of chocolate into our room, and Charles took Mr. P. some coffee into his. We had a very large Hackney coach ordered and somehow, in the pitch dark, we managed to pack into it all our bundles and trunks as well as Betty and our three selves.

Charlotte has travelled nowhere since she has been at the school and her excitement was delightful to behold. In the great yard at the Golden Cross, the lanterns and torches were flaring, and our breath was steaming in the frosty air. Charlotte's eyes were darting everywhere – as she drank in the scene of the shoving crowds, the shouting porters, and the crafty salesmen with their wares, whom I feel sure she could not have resisted had she had any money to spend. I was glad to observe that she kept a respectable distance between herself and the horses, who, even tho' held in check by the oslers, looked very wild, tossing their heads and snorting with impatience to be off.

We were about to take our places when an unexpected difficulty arose. Charles had not been able to secure a place inside for Charlotte, but we had hoped to remedy this when we actually came in person at the Yard. But it was not possible. Every seat was already disposed. I was very much concerned, but Charlotte, whose quiet manners give no indication of her sturdy, independent nature, declared that she was not a sailor's daughter for nothing, that she should enjoy the air and the view and the *adventure* of riding on the top. Besides, she said, she was often sick if she had to ride inside a stuffy coach. My imagination was full of dangerous possibilities: that she might fall off, or at the very least would catch a severe cold! I had on a thick stuff gown, so I lent her my warm pelisse, keeping for myself my fur tippet and charged Betty to look after her. I would have felt better if she could have sat beside the coachman, between him and the guard, but unfortunately that seat was already engaged by a sickly-looking boy, and she was obliged to sit on top facing backwards, four in a row, with Betty on one side and two rough men who were on their way to Bristol on the other.

I watched them climb safely up the ladder, then Mr. P. and I took our places. You can picture it all – the luggage bestowed, the swagman shouting, All Ready, the guard blowing his horn, the oslers throwing off the quarter cloths – the stately coachman flicking his reins, and then – we were away. – the four horses stepping out in perfect unison. As we left the yard, we passed the incoming coaches, dirty and travel-stained, arriving from distant parts of the kingdom. Even I felt the thrill of embarking on an adventure and did so wish I could have seen Charlotte's face. Surprising how it enhances one's *own* enjoyment to participate in the pleasure a young person is experiencing. But *you*, dear Mary, have known all about that for years.

Inside the coach Mr. P. and I had a large woman with a noisy baby and a quiet, muscular, foreign-looking young gentleman who sat in his corner and did not volunteer. Indeed, tired as we all were from the early start and the lack of sleep, joined with the darkness and the jolting and the noise, none of us were much disposed to conversation.

Our first stage was to Hounslow where the horses were changed. There, we went into the inn for breakfast. My first concern was to hear how Charlotte had fared. I stood and waited as she and Betty climbed down the ladder. She assured me that she *liked* riding up there, that my pelisse kept her very warm, her only inconvenience came from the Welshman beside her who would lean his head on her shoulder, while his hat poked into her face. But as she was sitting between him and Betty, I did not fear for her falling off, at least, and Betty is a strong, sensible young woman with her wits about her. I had been very vexed with Mr. P. for choosing to go in the coach instead of hiring a chaise, but at least he did not economize on victuals at the Inn. We were ushered into a private room, which he had ordered. Charlotte expressed surprise at how much he had to tip the coachman *and* the guard *and* the waiters.

"But observe, dear child," said he, "that by a liberal distribution of shillings we are receiving excellent service, have secured breakfast immediately and are able to warm ourselves by the fire, which more niggardly passengers will not be able to do, I assure you."

"But, sir, with respect, perhaps they cannot afford to disperse so many shillings?"

"Then unfortunately they must go cold and hungry."

She said no more. She has a kind heart, I am persuaded. All too soon the horn blew and we had to go out again. I watched Charlotte and Betty to the top, then climbed myself into the cold, noisy, stuffy coach. The baby was extremely fractious, and the mother would suckle it before us which exceedingly mortified Mr. Pinkney and the young gentleman, who kept their eyes resolutely toward the window. I did attempt some commonplace remarks, but they were not answered, and, indeed, the circumstances were hardly propitious for any sort of social exchange. Thus the weary day progressed, stage by stage, until we reached Chippenham, the last one before Bath, and *that* is where disaster nearly overtook us.

Fresh horses had been harnessed, and the horn had blown. Mr. Pinkney and the woman and baby were already settled inside, but I as usual waited, as I had done all along, to see Charlotte and Betty safely back up on their seat. Charlotte was climbing the ladder, was at the very top, was about to step into her place, when the stable lad holding the lead horse was distracted for a moment, and it, being fresh, started to move. The ladder toppled and Charlotte would have been been dashed onto the stony courtyard and very likely killed were it not for the presence of mind of our young gentleman, who being waiting behind me to take his place, with the greatest alertness sprang forward and caught her, breaking her fall, they both tumbling together onto the ground.

Imagine my distress. I was in an agony of fear. The coachman was shouting and pulling on the reins, the oslers leaping to catch the horses, the crowd surging forward in anticipation of some horrid sight, while I was trying in vain to reach Charlotte. She, however, was already being lifted up by the guard and porters, and with what relief did I see her able to stand, though white of face and trembling with shock. The coach now being brought to a halt a few yards from where we stood, Mr. P. was anxiously looking out of the door while I attempted to thank the young gentleman, who protested that it was nothing, though his clothes were disordered and his hat battered. It was his hat, I believe, which saved his head.

This heroic person now insisted on giving up his seat inside to Charlotte, which I very gratefully accepted, you may be sure. She was too shaken to say a word. I did ask him if he, after such a fall, would be equal to sitting on top, but he assured me he had had worse tumbles than that, and was very strong, and he climbed up the ladder before another word could be said. There was not time for more, the coachman was anxious to be off, as this little accident had delayed us by several minutes, and he would be late clocking in to Bath.

Mr. P., fortunately, had a flask of brandy with him, and under its influence Charlotte gradually revived. We agreed that as soon as we reached the White Hart, we would speak to the young man and thank him properly. Mr. P. wondered if he would accept any reimbursement for the mending of his clothes. *I* wondered if we might not invite him to dine with us. But in the confusion and bustle of our arrival, and the circumstance of the woman with the baby pushing forward and preventing us getting out of the coach, our young benefactor was down from the top, had collected his belongings and was gone before we could even catch sight of him.

We were very much distressed. We have no way to thank him, and we know nothing about him; only that he informed Betty while sitting beside her on the top, that he is in the navy, and that when he was a midshipman he had twice fallen off the rigging onto the deck. We *presume* he is staying in Bath.

Charlotte was excessively disappointed. Even a young lady who does *not* read novels would find such an encounter promising. But since there was nothing to be done, after a comfortable supper we went to bed, and, as I have already indicated, happily Charlotte does not seem to have suffered any lasting ill-effects from her fall.

"Oh, I am quite well, thank you, madam," said she in answer to my inquiry this morning. "Very stiff, and quite covered in bruises, but aside from that, very well."

"Aside from that!" I exclaimed. "I believe you ought to be staying in bed, young lady."

"Oh, no, madam," she hastily replied, "please do not make me. I could not bear to waste a precious minute of our time in Bath."

"Well," said I, seeing how earnestly she desired to go out, and thinking how wonderful it was to be young and resilient, "if it is only bruises, I suppose they will fade in time."

"Yes, indeed," said she, "please do not worry on my account. But I *do* wonder about the young gentleman. *He* fell directly on the ground."

"My dear," said I, "judging by the alacrity with which he left the coach last night he was not in the least incapacitated, besides, he was wearing a thick greatcoat with many capes and I am sure that protected him."

"I wonder if we will ever see him again?" said she, a little wistfully.

"I cannot say, my dear," said I.

"Anyway, he would never look at me with my hair."

The poor child. Her red hair is really her despair.

"Cheer up, my dear," said I smiling. "Many people *like* red hair, and it is *possible* we may meet him at the Pump-room or in Sidney Gardens. But come, let us think about our shopping. The maid told me there is a fine dimity to be had in Milsom Street, and you have your five guineas to spend."

Thus did I pass off the subject, and I hope that she will put the young man out of her head, for, although we might meet him accidentally, she certainly cannot depend upon it, or that he should wish to continue the acquaintance if we did. For the moment, the delights of being at an inn – and not at school – and the prospect of money to spend must be her consolation.

She is sitting beside me now writing out lists of what she might purchase, and five guineas, carefully contrived, will go a good way towards acquiring some pretty gowns.

Here is the waiter just come with our breakfast. This letter is already too long; but I shall send it to the post at once, so that it arrives in time to send you my very best wishes for Christmas.

Yours very affectionately,
Charlotte

P.S. Thank you for the receipt for chilblains. Fortunately, although there is a severe frost, this inn is kept decently warm. But I will see that it is made up by our cook for Charlotte when she returns to school in two weeks' time.

LETTER 19

From Mrs. Goddard to Mrs. Pinkney

Highbury,
24 December 1813

My dearest Charlotte,

Your letter has just this minute come by the second post. Such an alarming accident you tell me of. What a guardian angel that young man turned out to be! The most terrible tragedy, indeed, if your kindness to this young woman should have resulted in her death. One reads of so many coaching accidents these days, it almost makes one afraid to travel.

Well, well, when there is a young person under one's care, it is indeed a care, which I am myself feeling more than usually at this moment.

Harriet came back from Hartfield last night with a cold and a bad sore throat. It is a weakness to which she has been subject ever since she was a little girl. On this occasion she probably caught it from Sukey.

In spite of being feverish and retired to bed, she was nonetheless quite determined to take up a dinner invitation this evening to Mr. Weston's; but she is absolutely unfit to go out and I have had to be adamant. The poor child was bitterly disappointed and wept and wept. I cannot account for her being so set upon going to this party. It is only at Randalls, the other guests are to be only Mr. and Miss Woodhouse, Mr. Knightley, and Mr. and Mrs. John Knightley. With the exception of the last-named, these are all people whom she sees almost every day – ever since I introduced her at Hartfield. Oh, I forgot Mr. Elton! He is invited also. Oh dear, can *he* be the cause? Mercy on us, given all that has happened, I suppose he is!

Since I last wrote on the subject I have heard from Harriet that Mr. Elton, himself, insisted upon taking her picture up to London to be framed. So you were right, dear Charlotte. It was, indeed, the "exceedingly precious" object. No wonder she was puffed up at the news. I have now seen this famous portrait hanging on the wall in the drawing-room at Hartfield. It is quite a tolerable likeness, except that Miss Woodhouse has made her too tall, and her eyebrows and eyelashes too dark.

So here she is, on Christmas Eve, in bed and miserable. Miss Woodhouse has been so good as to come and sit with her; she is upstairs now. It is of considerable assistance to me since I have many calls upon my time, and really have no business to be writing to you! But I did want to reach you, if possible, before Christmas Day, and to send my sympathies on Charlotte's accident. The last of the girls are returning to their homes, and there is much bustle and confusion of trunks and parents and horses. But I have been up since six, and feel entitled to a brief respite. For the moment Alice and John and the three teachers are quite equal to the occasion.

I have just been upstairs to thank Miss Woodhouse, and found her in a chair close beside Harriet's bed. "Pray, Miss Woodhouse," said I, "do not sit so near, I beg you. You would not want to catch Harriet's cold." Miss Woodhouse replied that she never took cold, was always in excellent health. Is it not strange, Charlotte, but I got the impression that colds were a weakness entirely beneath her notice!

I had to break off there, to say goodbye to the girls. It looks as if it might snow, and a few flakes are falling. I also saw Miss Woodhouse from the door. As she left, Mr. Elton approached and met her just outside. I believe he was coming to inquire after Harriet – that is the kind of obliging, pleasant attention which makes him such a very popular young man. I am sure Miss Nash fancies him, I caught her peeping through the window curtains. She and Miss Prince often take their walk along Vicarage Lane, it was they who first remarked on the yellow curtains.

But I digress – I watched Mr. Elton and Miss Woodhouse talking in the road together, then along came Mr. John Knightley with his two eldest boys and the party moved off towards Hartfield. Some people wonder if Mr. Elton and Miss Woodhouse would not make a match. Mrs. Cole and Miss Bates were talking of it the other day. Certainly it is a pity that such an elegant, handsome young woman does not marry, though I do not know what in the world would become of poor Mr. Woodhouse if she did. Well, well, I must stop gossiping and get on with my jobs.

Christmas Day: 8 a.m.

I could not get this posted yesterday, and now we have four inches of snow! Luckily it fell during the night. I am glad it did not fall yesterday, or the girls would not have been able to get off. I could not finish my letter before, what with nursing Harriet and settling a dispute in the kitchen as to who should stuff the turkey. I resolved it by declaring that they could pull straws, one could make the stuffing and the other the brandy sauce for the pudding. Sarah, my cook, has enough to do without attending to these extra tasks. The three teachers all stay here for the holidays, none of them having any other settled home but this, and Miss Bickerton, also, as well as four or five younger children who live too far off or whose parents are abroad. I have been overseeing fires and making sure the water in the jugs does not freeze. John is taking this now to the post office. I very much doubt that we shall be able to get to church today. Harriet is no better and is keeping her bed.

Belated greetings,

Yours affectionately,

M. Goddard

LETTER 20

From Mrs. Pinkney to Mrs. Goddard

The White Hart
Bath
27 December 1813

My dear Mary,

Early morning, and your letter has just come. What changes for Harriet! Two months ago she was in awe of an invitation to Hartfield, and now she has her likeness adorning the wall of the drawing room! It is enough to turn a much stronger head than hers.

I hope you had an agreeable Christmas, even if you were snowed in. But with good fires and good books and plenty of turkey and plum pudding, nothing could be pleasanter if the company is congenial, which, dear Mary, knowing your capacity for friendship and for making the people about you happy, I am sure must have been the case.

So you and Mrs. Cole and Miss Bates have been arranging that Mr. Elton should marry Miss Woodhouse, have you? Yet Harriet is in love with him, evidently, and Miss Nash, also, as well as innumerable other females. He must be a most charming young man. Very sad for the young ladies of Highbury whenever he *does* marry, then all the fun and speculation and courting games must come to a close.

Well, we shall soon have been here a week. Mr. P. has been taking the waters with some good effect. In the evenings, while he and the Admiral have been at their chess and their port (in moderation in his case, Mr. P. assures me) Charlotte and I have taken ourselves to various entertainments. Contrary to our original expectations (and to her extreme disappointment) we have seen neither hide nor hair of the young naval gentleman. She mentions him almost every day, and wonders where he is and how he does, and how it is we can never have encountered him in any of the public places. He has certainly caught her imagination. Hardly surprising, given the dramatic circumstances, and the poor child has almost no one else to care for or to think about.

Admiral Seymour joined us for Christmas dinner. It was the first time I had actually sat down with the gentleman. He is a bluff and hearty person, a little overbearing, to be sure, with a sailor's weather-beaten complexion. His first sally to me was, "Well, madam, I never thought any woman would tempt my old bachelor friend to give up his freedom, but you did. What is your secret?"

And upon my disclaiming, (rather embarrassed) he followed this opening by inquiring, "And how does marriage to Pinkney suit you?" I was a little taken aback, you may be sure, but I answered, "Very well, I thank you, sir." I saw him looking at me quizzically. Mr. P. was busy carving the turkey, and either did not hear, or did not choose to hear, thus the subject was dropped. The Admiral, himself, has buried two wives, I understand.

Still, withal, he is very likeable in his way and with him Mr. P. quite blooms in conversation. They have known each other since they were boys growing up in the same village where the Admiral's father was the squire, and Mr. P.'s the parson. I had thought that the Admiral might have know Mr. Grenville, but no. Mr. G.'s and Mr. P.'s acquaintance stems from their days at Cambridge together, by which time the Admiral was already a lieutenant at sea. I have always found sailors to be excellent raconteurs and the Admiral was no exception having many curious anecdotes to relate. Charlotte quite hung upon his words. This led to my mentioning that her own father had been in the navy. The melancholy circumstance of the disappearance of the *Penelope* was well-known to him, Charlotte then expressed the hope that her father might still be alive.

"Is it not possible, sir? Like Robinson Crusoe?"

"Or Alexander Selkirk?" smiled the Admiral, and he was so kind as to concede that it was not beyond the bounds of possibility and that survivors have been known to be marooned on remote islands for several years.

To dispel the gloom which naturally followed this conversation, the Admiral remarked to her in his joking way,

"But, child, you must feel pretty marooned yourself, shut up with these two old folks."

"No, indeed, sir," she replied with spirit, "it is a great deal better than school, I assure you. I am very glad to be here with Mr. and Mrs. Pinkney."

"Besides," said I, "I do not consider myself *old*, Admiral, it is not very gallant of you, sir."

"No," said Mr. P., "you must remember that Mrs. Pinkney is some years younger than we are."

"My apologies, madam," said he with a bow, "I was only speaking relatively, compared to Miss Gordon, that is," and turning to Charlotte he said, "I expect you enjoy the Assemblies? A pretty young lady like you will have all kinds of partners, I'll be bound?"

"Alas, no, sir," said she, with disarming frankness. "I wish I had. For although Mrs. Pinkney and I have been to every Assembly, we have not been introduced to *a single soul*."

"Indeed? It does not sound as if the Master of Ceremonies was performing his office."

"It is very provoking," said I. "If we knew even *one* person, we might easily meet others."

"You forget, madam," said Charlotte, "that we have met *one* young gentleman."

"But my dear Charlotte," said I, "we are not even certain that he is staying in Bath."

The Admiral, bemused, looked as if he hardly knew what to make of this, but before he could speak, Charlotte began again.

"Perhaps, sir, you may have heard of him? He is in the navy."

"Quite possible, if I knew his name?"

"That is the difficulty," said she, "we do not know it."

The Admiral laughed incredulously.

"I wish we did," I said. "I believe it is not too much to say that he saved Charlotte's life." And I proceeded to give particulars of the incident.

"Ah, yes," said the Admiral, "I believe Pinkney did just mention it to me."

"I did more than mention it," said Mr. P. "I told you the whole story, that first day, after we arrived."

"I fear I did not pay that much attention," said the Admiral. "I should have done so had I realized it was a *sailor* who rendered you this service. Most commendable. Prompt action. True naval alacrity. Well, I wonder that this young gallant has not called upon you, at the very least to inquire how you did?"

"We hoped that he might," said Charlotte, who is unaffected and straight-forward to a fault.

The Admiral laughed and said he hoped so, too, and made us promise to introduce the young gentleman if he ever did appear. Poor child, I wish she could meet someone her own age. Here she has two new gowns to wear, and no partner with whom to dance.

Adieu,

Charlotte

LETTER 20, continued

From Mrs. Pinkney to Mrs. Goddard

The White Hart
Bath
27 December 1813

Do not be surprised, my dear Mary, that I am writing to you again, twice in one day. I do not wish to be too heavy a drain on your purse, but since the post office is so extremely efficient, and even here in Bath there are so many mails a day, why not take advantage of it? We have finished dinner, Mr. Pinkney is with the

Admiral, and Charlotte is dressing her hair. So while I am waiting for the hour of setting out for the Rooms, I thought I would write. You never expected to hear from me so often, did you? But I am longing to tell you – you with all the would-be romantic affairs you are able to report of your Harriet, that, finally, the young sailor has tacked into view on Charlotte's horizon.

This morning, after I had already posted my previous letter to you, *he* called at last. Charlotte and I were in our sitting room with Betty busy about her new gowns, matching ribbons, adding lace, and so forth. I was wishing once again that she had someone to wear them for, when, lo and behold, there was a little bustle and Lieutenant Marlowe was announced! Betty hastily gathered up the clothes and made her exit, but not before the young man acknowledged her very graciously. It was from Betty, when they had sat together on top of the coach, that he had learned our names, though neglecting to tell her his.

Lieutenant Richard Marlowe has a darkish complexion, brown eyes, prominent black eyebrows and very white teeth. He has, in fact, quite a Spanish appearance. He does not smile often, but when he does his face lights up most attractively. He obviously is more used to the quarter deck than the drawing room, but he apologised most sincerely for not calling sooner: the friends with whom he is staying had a visiting elderly parent over Christmas to whom attention had to be paid. His concern for the effects of Charlotte's fall were obviously genuine. He had, unknown to us, actually sent his friends' servant to inquire of the innkeeper how she did. I could see that this attention was much felt by Charlotte.

At first, to be sure, the burden of keeping the conversation going between these two young people fell chiefly upon me. Charlotte, having lived exclusively among females for two years, is a little bashful in the company of men; but although her tongue was silent her eyes spoke eloquently.

We were talking of the weather and the Christmas season, and it was not until Lieutenant Marlowe was explaining how, until the elderly visitor left, he had not been at liberty to attend any of the Assemblies, that I remembered my promise to the Admiral.

"There is someone who wishes to meet you, sir," said I. "Admiral Seymour is the gentleman's name."

The young man started. "Not Admiral *Richard* Seymour?"

"I believe that is his Christian name. He is with Mr. Pinkney at this moment, and if you will excuse me, I shall fetch them." I stepped along the passage to where they were drinking coffee.

"Mr. Pinkney," said I, "I have someone with me whose acquaintance I believe both yourself and the Admiral would like to make."

With only a few grumbles the two gentlemen followed me to our room, where I had the pleasure of providing a much greater surprise than any of us could have imagined.

Because, while Mr. P. was attempting to express thanks and gratitude to Lieutenant Marlowe, the Admiral was cutting him off and almost pushing him aside as he exclaimed loudly, "Not Lieutenant *Richard* Marlowe? Is it possible that you are the son of Captain Frederick Marlowe?"

"I am, indeed, sir."

"For sixteen years I have wondered what became of you," said the Admiral, warmly shaking hands. "Your father was serving with me in Spain when you were born."

"So I have been told, sir."

"Although our two countries were not at war at the time, I considered it very ill-advised of him to marry a Spanish woman, be she ever so beautiful and charming."

"I believe she was, sir. Though I hardly remember my mother. She died in childbed when I was barely five years old."

"But of course I am very well aware of that fact."

"Indeed, sir?"

"It was in '98. Shortly afterwards your father was killed at Abukir Bay, our gallant Nelson's first glorious victory. You might have grown up a Roman Catholic, you know. You can thank me, young man, that you did not."

Lieutenant Marlowe bowed. "I have been told it was you who insisted on my being christened on board."

"Precisely. A Protestant," said the Admiral, "or you could never have joined the Royal Navy. You are my godson, you know, you were named after me."

"I am honoured, sir."

The Admiral looked him up and down. "When last I saw you, you were a pitiful orphan, ragged and unwanted. God knows what would have become of you if I had not arranged for a brother officer of your father's to take you home to England."

"I would have grown up a Spanish street urchin," smiled Lieutenant Marlowe.

"If you'd grown up at all," remarked the Admiral.

"I remember the voyage back to England well," said the young man. "I was five years old and I spoke no English."

"But at that age – you soon learned."

Lieutenant Marlowe laughed. "Now I speak no Spanish. I do not imagine my English grandparents were too pleased to have an unknown foreign stray landed on their doorstep."

"Nonsense, man, it was their plain duty to take you in. It had been a legal marriage, after all."

"Well, sir, at least they had the goodness to keep me until I was twelve years old and could be sent to the naval academy."

"And what better place for a likely lad?"

"None that I know of, sir."

The Admiral smiled indulgently at this correct response so promptly given. I tell you, Mary, that to those of us who were listening, the young man's history seemed almost as wonderful as a tale from the Arabian nights. I shall not soon forget Charlotte's eyes fixed upon his face.

"It was my great regret," the Admiral continued, "that I myself did not return to England for several years, and when I did I was embroiled in domestic difficulties of my own. As your godfather, I ought to have searched you out. But you could the more easily have found me, young man. I might have been of use to you."

"I suppose, sir, I thought I ought to make my own way."

The Admiral appeared not displeased at this reply.

"Which you have done, and without interest?"

"I served my six years as a mid, sir, then I passed for lieutenant."

"Before your twenty-first birthday?" chided the Admiral.

"Ah, you've caught me out there, sir."

"Well, well, that rule was often waived in times of war. I understand you saved this young lady from being dashed to the ground."

"I happened to be standing in the right place at the right time, sir."

"He's too modest," I cried.

"Indeed!" exclaimed Mr. Pinkney.

Even Charlotte was unable to resist chiming in, anxious that Lieutenant Marlowe should receive all the credit due to him. "He actually saved my life," she declared smiling at him shyly.

"Yet this is the first time you have come to see how the young lady did?" said the Admiral. "Shame on you!"

"I did not wish to put myself forward, sir."

"Oh, fiddle dee dee! You put yourself forward in action, evidently. A little more endeavour in the drawing room, if you please. A sailor must be ready to navigate in all waters, you know."

So they quizzed each other and chatted on in this manner very pleasantly. Lieutenant Marlowe is evidently not much more than one and twenty, but, having been at sea since he was fourteen, does not lack confidence when speaking of his profession. On being questioned by the Admiral he talked of his ships and his travels. He has just come back from America where he took part in the blockade of the eastern ports. They spoke of a battle off Boston earlier this year, when the U.S.S. *Chesapeake* met the H.M.S. *Shannon*. Imagine, dear Mary, in an engagement of only eleven minutes more men were killed than in the whole of the Battle of Trafalgar. They agreed the Americans were "rattling good sailors".

He has been up the St. Lawrence River as far as Montreal. I said I did not realize Montreal was on a river, and they all had a good laugh at my expense. The men then spoke about the ship-building on Lake Erie. (I did not admit I did not know exactly where that was, either.) The British and the Americans each aim to build bigger and bigger vessels, apparently. Whoever is behindhand dares not venture out of port. Now Lieutenant Marlowe's own ship is home for refit. He is turned ashore on half-pay and is not very happy about it, I gather.

Charlotte, being a sailor's daughter, actually knew where all the places he mentioned were. Her father had been to America, and they had made a practice at home of looking at maps. Next time I can lay my hands upon an atlas, I must refresh my memory. The young gentleman stayed a full hour; before he left we made arrangements to meet in the rooms this evening.

I am so pleased for Charlotte's sake. Since she is *my* "Harriet" I simply had to write and tell you.

Adieu,

C. Pinkney

LETTER 21

From Mrs. Goddard to Mrs. Pinkney

Highbury,
29 December 1813

Do you really not know where Montreal is? Or Lake Erie? My dear sister! I am quite astonished. You should be required to attend my school and learn a little Geography.

I am delighted by what you tell me of young Charlotte. I hope she has much felicity and no heartbreak from acquaintance with the young man, who does seem to come from a most unusual background.

As you surmised, we had a pleasant Christmas, in spite of, or perhaps I should say because of, the snow. Good fires, good food, good company. Now our already small circle in Highbury is shrinking further. Mr. and Mrs. John Knightley returned yester-day to town, and Mr. Elton, to everyone's surprise and without the smallest previous hint or warning, has today taken himself off to Bath. Undoubtedly the labours of his profession are great at this season of the year and he deserves a respite, but still, it seems a decision suddenly made. How amusing it would be if you should happen to fall in with him there.

Then Mr. Frank Churchill, who was finally to have honoured the whole of Highbury by his long-promised visit to his father, has once again sent a letter of excuse. His aunt's health was given as the reason. Poor Mrs. Weston. She says nothing, of course, but I am convinced she is secretly mortified that he does not think it worth his while to make this trifling effort on her behalf; three months as they have now been married, too! We know he was at Weymouth in October where he met Miss Fairfax (Miss Bates's niece, you remember) with Colonel and Mrs. Campbell and their daughter. If he can contrive Weymouth, why not Highbury? Surely his aunt is not so unreasonable or in such poor health as all that? These delays and excuses are paying Mrs. Weston no compliment, and in my opinion do not speak too highly of the principles of the young man either.

My poor little Harriet is recovering from her cold. For a few days I was really anxious about her. This morning Miss Woodhouse came to call – the first time since Christmas Eve; for until this thaw, the weather has made visiting impossible. She looked very grave, and going into Harriet's bedroom, closed the door behind her.

Miss Nash, who happened to be upstairs at the time, told me she heard Miss Woodhouse's voice going on and on in a monologue, without Harriet uttering a single word, and then Harriet sobbing! What can this be about? The idea that Miss Woodhouse would deliberately give pain to her little friend is inconceivable.

Some time later, after she had gone, I went in to speak to Harriet about her washing, and found her lying on her bed with a red and swollen face. I asked her what was the matter; she said it was nothing, she had a headache and would like to be alone. She spoke of Mr. Elton's departure for Bath, of which, apparently, Miss Woodhouse had apprised her. Poor child! She has been completely obsessed with him, lately. His going certainly confirms that he cannot be in love with *her* however much she may be in love with *him*. She never speaks of the Martins now. How the "Courtship" conundrum and the thing "exceedingly precious" fit in to all this, I have not patience to determine.

She is going to stay at Hartfield for a few days, and I hope that will improve her spirits.

Yours aff:ly,

M. G.

LETTER 22

From Mrs. Pinkney to Mrs. Goddard

White Hart
Bath
4 January 1814

It is not a reproach to *me*, I hope, dear Mary, your remarks about Mr. Frank Churchill being unable or unwilling to visit Highbury. You know how dearly I would love to come, if only it were in my power.

Of course I am always diverted by your news of that inimitable place – as I *now* think of it. You are aware, I believe, that I never met either Mr. or Mrs. Churchill at Enscombe; they dined only with the great families; nor have I heard anything of them since our friend ceased to tutor the young man. But surely, unreasonable and difficult as she is known to be, Mrs. Churchill would not, *could* not keep him from visiting his own father? I cannot forbear to observe that were your Mrs. Weston a woman of consequence, means would be found to effect this visit.

As to Harriet Smith, you say her tears were caused by what Miss Woodhouse had to tell her behind the closed door. What do you suppose that was? It cannot have been only that Mr. Elton was leaving for Bath? *His* sudden departure is very suspicious. Harriet has had all the encouragement of the "Courtship" charade as well as the mention to Mr. Perry of the thing "exceedingly precious," to foster her falling in love with him, or, at the very least, to fancy *him* in love with her. Her disappointment at missing the Westons' dinner party on Christmas Eve was understandable, but her excessive grief, surely was disproportionate to the occasion? If she were *secure* of him, she should not have been so overpowered. No, it looks like Harriet was no part of Mr. Elton's design, however much *he* was of hers.

Well, well, now he has gone to Bath. She will have to fix on some other object to occupy what passes for her mind. Oh dear, you are not going to like that remark, dear Mary; but I will not scratch it out and ruin the page, because I suppose even you must acknowledge the truth of it.

More to the point, why did he leave Highbury so precipitately? It was obviously an object with him to be gone and very speedily, too. I strongly suspect it is something to do with Miss Woodhouse. From visiting Hartfield *every* day, he is now to visit it not at all. Could he have made her an offer and been refused? Well, it is all guesswork and conjecture, but you know how I love to wrestle with these puzzles.

So, given all the preceeding, it amuses me excessively to report that this famous Don Juan of yours has arrived here, and that we have made his acquaintance already.

But that is to anticipate. You will have to wait in suspense, because to keep my narrative in chronological order I must first tell you about our evening at the rooms. Charlotte looked very appealing in her new white muslin gown with emerald green ribbons. Her eyes were actually shining with excitement. Before we left, I said to her, "You look very pretty, my dear. I am sure Lieutenant Marlowe will think so, too." Well, you might suppose I had given her a thousand pounds in gold coin the way the child's face lit up. Who would have thought that a simple compliment could do so much for the self-esteem of a poor young lady? She confessed she had never in her life before been told she looked pretty.

"What?" cried I, "not even by your own mother?"

"My mother was always so very sick," said she. "Besides, I was not pretty, but very plain."

"I cannot dispute that," said I, "for I did not know you then. But believe me, my dear, you are very pretty now."

She seemed quite disinclined to believe me. Is that not sad, my dear Mary? I shall certainly make a point of praising her as much as possible in the future.

We arrived at the rooms and at first *he* did not appear. The place was crowded, but it was not long before we saw him across the floor. He was with a pleasant, sensible-looking couple, whom I imagined to be Navy, also. Directly he caught sight of us, he came over, bowed, and claimed Charlotte's hand, for the music was just beginning. It was with great satisfaction that I watched them. Two young people with so much in common: orphans, the Navy, both unaffected and honest – it would be strange, indeed, if they did not take to each other. They danced twice together before tea, and then Lieutenant Marlowe left early with his friends. I believe the wife is with child. When we got back to the Inn, Charlotte exclaimed,

"Oh, Mrs. Pinkney, I never met a young man that I *liked* so much before."

"I am glad, my dear, very glad," said I, trying to keep my countenance, for how many young men has she ever met? They could be counted on one hand, I feel sure.

But you are wanting to hear about Mr. Elton, and I will keep you waiting no longer. He came on the 30th, having spent a night in town with his mother and sisters, as he subsequently told us. And how did we meet him, I hear you asking? Well, as the evening arrival of the coach at the White Hart is a sight which always rejoices the spirit – the sounding horn, the steaming horses, the bustle of new arrivals; if we are at leisure, my young friend and I make it a point to be on hand to watch. Indeed, I am glad to have the excuse of her entertainment to do so, because I really enjoy it very much myself! Thus it was that we saw the trunk thrown off, inscribed, *The Rev. Philip Elton, White-*

Hart, Bath. We then perceived the owner, himself, claiming it. A pretty-looking fellow with an eye for the ladies, I should say.

I was determined to introduce myself when the occasion offered, and luckily it came about almost immediately and without any scheming or impropriety on my part. Charlotte and I, if we do not go to the rooms or the theatre, frequently enjoy a late supper in the dining room of the inn where we can watch the company. Having been at the Assembly the previous night, on this occasion we were staying in – especially as we had heard that Lieutenant Marlowe and his friends were otherwise engaged. Mr. P. being with the Admiral as usual, Charlotte and I were alone. A waiter had put the dish we had ordered – creamed sole – on Mr. Elton's table, and given us his beef steak and oysters. Expostulations and apologies ensued. Thinking partly of you, and partly of Charlotte and how agreeable it would be for her to have as many young acquaintance as possible in this place, (to say nothing of my own curiosity) I was so bold as to speak to him thus:

"Pardon me, sir, but do I have the honour of addressing Mr. Elton?"

He expressed surprise at my knowing his name. I spoke of the trunk, and very soon the word *Highbury* came into the conversation. I said I was the sister of Mrs. Goddard, who must be well-known to him. Mr. Elton bowed and I thought his smile became a little frozen at my mention of the place and your name. He inquired when I had last visited there. I replied that I had never been in Highbury in my life nor had I ever met any of the inhabitants. His smile broadened and I got the impression he was distinctly relieved. Why should this be so? What has he to conceal? Does he think I might be a voluntary spy on behalf of someone there? Miss Woodhouse, for example? Or Harriet Smith?

Do not be alarmed, dear Mary, I speak partly in jest, and you can count on me not to breathe a word of anything you have ever told me, and, indeed, I am more likely to entrap information by not doing so. Now do not pretend to be shocked, I beg you. My interest is in people, and all I can learn about their vagaries and peculiarities diverts me excessively: a harmless amusement, especially as I have no one to whom I can or do repeat what I learn but you. And who knows? I may discover something very entertaining.

Mr. Elton is to remain only a few nights here at the White Hart. Some friends with whom he was to stay being occupied with other guests at present. We chatted about the usual commonplaces of strangers, the shocking condition of the public coaches, how often they overturned, the dangers of travel, the state of the roads, etc., moving by gradual degrees to the many and various entertainments to be found in Bath. Dare I repeat to you what the villain said? That the theatres, concerts, dancing, and music of this place were what he was looking forward to with great anticipation: a most welcome change, said he, from the whist club at Highbury! What say you to that?

Such a wretch, so to impugn your lovely Highbury. Charlotte took some part in the conversation, but seemed distracted. I believe her mind was fixed more upon the gallant lieutenant than on the reverend cleric. Mr. Elton, however, was evidently so much pleased with our acquaintance as to ask if we would be attending the Master of Ceremonies Ball the next evening, and if so, could he engage Miss Gordon for the first dance?

Here was a slight difficulty. I saw Charlotte hesitating. We had told Lieutenant Marlowe that we would be there, but since she was not positively engaged there was no reason to refuse Mr. Elton, and before she might do so, I spoke up for her. "Miss Gordon will be charmed, will you not, Charlotte?" Later she reproached me gently. "My dear," said I, "a little competition never did any woman a disservice."

And so it was. I was rejoiced to see Charlotte enjoying the attentions of *two* young men. Lieutenant Marlowe and his friends appeared shortly after the music had commenced. Charlotte was already dancing with Mr. Elton. I watched with the triumph of a strategist the expression on Lieutenant Marlowe's face when he saw her. He soon claimed the next dance, however, and in addition, praise be, an introduction came from the Master of Ceremonies at last. So she had a variety of partners on which to ring the changes. I have never seen her so animated. One thing that Seminary has taught her well is how to dance; light as a feather and a pleasure to watch.

I was really very proud of Charlotte: felt quite like a mother hen with her chick. At tea, Lieutenant Marlowe was obliged to join his friends, so we sat with Mr. Elton. I attempted to speak to him about Highbury, but that seemed a subject distasteful to him. He was more interested in asking our advice and opinion as to how he could make the most of his time in Bath. Even as we were talking I could see his eyes roaming round the room. In search of what? I asked myself. Why is he here? You see how this little mystery intrigues me.

Charlotte, in the chaise going home, said she had had a charming evening, but that she wished Mr. Elton might leave her alone in future. With all due respect to the young ladies of Highbury, she declared that she found his studying to please insincere: that his agreeing to everything she said with his "Exactly so" drove her to distraction; the open decisive manners of Lieutenant Marlowe, who would contradict or disagree if he felt like it in true naval style, were much more to her taste. I am pleased that she has gained so much in confidence since she has been with us. Being away from that dreadful school, being properly fed, well-dressed, and associating with people who cosset and praise her has worked wonders.

I find these flirtations among the young people vastly entertaining. After Charlotte had gone to bed, Mr. P. and I sat for a long time over a glass of claret (with water in his case) and I regaled him with the evening's adventures, in which he took a genuine interest. He seemed in a very good humour and more willing to converse than he ever has been before. He voluntarily mentioned Mr. Grenville's name, and remarked how much he had enjoyed his society when they were undergraduates together at Cambridge. "But I was a different person, then," he said with a sigh. I did not inquire what he meant by this. He was certainly *younger*! He is much more cheerful and his gout is better, though it has meant denying himself the plum puddings and rich roasts and brandy on which he loves to feast at this season of the year.

After our talk, I ventured to say to him, "Mr. Pinkney, why do you not leave your chess? You miss so much, hiding yourself away in your room and filling your brain with moves and counter moves. Come out and see how the world goes round."

"One of these days," said he, "perhaps I shall."

Unfortunately we return to town very soon.

Adieu,

Charlotte

LETTER 23

From Mrs. Goddard to Mrs. Pinkney

Highbury,
8 January 1814

My dear Charlotte,

I do not think our ideas of *propriety* quite coincide. I am sure our mother would not have considered it very proper for two ladies to lounge about waiting for the coach to come in. Nor, actually to address a gentleman without a formal introduction. Ah well, you have always flouted convention, and there is little hope of your reformation now.

Aside from *that*, I am excessively diverted by what you have to report. How shocked the females in this school would be if they were to hear Charlotte's opinion of their idol! To them, Mr. Elton is the very standard of perfection: but in Highbury there are almost no eligible and handsome young men to be found compared to the vast numbers that I daresay populate the ballrooms and Pump-Rooms of Bath. As for your remark about Harriet, I have never claimed that she had a *mind*, only that she had a sweet, docile and grateful *disposition*, which surely (of the two) might be preferable in a *wife*, especially if the husband is a practical man of action and not overburdened with intellect himself. I am thinking of Robert Martin. Much good may it do me!

Your argument concluding Miss Woodhouse is the cause of Mr. Elton's leaving Highbury is very ingenious. Well, I doubt if we shall ever discover the truth.

Meanwhile I have many cares and concerns, which I shall not burden you with, except to say that this morning I had words with my trusty servant, Alice, who seems out of sorts these days. She has always been so even-tempered and reliable, I cannot account for it. I have had to remove little Sukey from her care. But Sukey is doing very much better, I am pleased to say. She is actually sitting opposite me now: practising her writing on her slate. It did not suit her father to have her at home for Christmas.

To compose myself following this rencontre with Alice, I determined to get out of the house for a short while and call on my old friends, the good Bateses.

I found Miss Bates quite in a state of ecstasy. She had just that morning had a letter from her niece Jane Fairfax, which she insisted upon reading aloud to me. Jane is proposing to pay them a long visit while Colonel and Mrs. Cambell are in Ireland with their newly-married daughter. I think I have mentioned, have I not, that Jane was taken into their family by the Campbells a few years after the death of her parents. She has received, therefore, a more superior education and up-bringing than her aunt and grandmother – widow of our former vicar – could ever have contrived for her.

This young woman is their darling and pride, and indeed, who can begrudge them their adoration of one so elegant and talented? The poor things live over a shop up a cramped and narrow staircase, and have little of comfort in their meagre quarters. Jane Fairfax will be a charming addition to our Highbury society at this dreary time of year.

I arrived at the Bateses hard on the heels of Miss Woodhouse and Harriet, who had just been to call: an unusual circumstance. In my opinion Miss Woodhouse does not call as often as she ought on these worthy people – but on this occasion she seems to have stayed a respectable length of time and gave much pleasure by praising Miss Fairfax's handwriting.

What a pity you have to return to London, just when Charlotte is beginning to enjoy herself. I respect your young lady for
not being overwhelmed by Mr. Elton's charms. Speaking of her
pleasure in your calling her pretty, certainly the best gift you can
bestow upon her is faith in herself. But I am sure you know that.
Sometime I should like to meet your Charlotte, but that is not
very likely to come about since I cannot even meet *you*, my dearest
sister.

Yours aff:ly,

M. Goddard

LETTER 24

From Mrs. Pinkney to Mrs. Goddard

White Hart

Bath

14 January 1814

My dear Mary,

We did not return to London, after all. Mr. P., to the joy of
Charlotte and myself, declared that we would defer our departure
yet again.

He is improved in health, is entertained by the company of
Charlotte, and enjoys the society of the Admiral. He has actually
left the chess board and come out with us on several occasions.
He says had he known we were to stay so long, he should have
taken lodgings. I am glad, however, that we did not. I confess the
liveliness and bustle of the Inn suits me. Every week Mr. Pinkney
says shall be our last, and every week he changes his mind. Lord
knows, *I* have no objection. I suppose we shall stay till the money
runs out. I have written twice to Madame Dubois to extend
Charlotte's time away from the Seminary.

The poor child asked me the other day if I thought Gowland's lotion would help her freckles. "But your freckles are charming," I said. "They are in keeping with your face and hair."

She blushed and said she did not know if Lieutenant Marlowe cared for freckles. "Well," said I, "he has a very dark complexion, himself. Almost swarthy one might call it. And people often like the opposite of what they are themselves. Anyway, your freckles do not seem to hinder your having many enjoyable excursions with him."

She acknowledged the truth of this. Indeed, they seem to be always together. I am rejoiced to note her looking so blooming. One could almost say radiant. With colour in her cheeks her red hair does not look so flaming, and in any case it is most distinctive. In spite of the time of year, the young people have been on many excursions around Bath, some by chaise and some on foot: Blaize Castle, Clifton, Charlcombe, Claverton Down, Bristol, and a long walk round Beechen Cliff. Fear not for the proprieties, dear sister. They are chaperoned occasionally by me, but more often by a charming Captain Adams, and, if the expedition is not too strenuous, by Mrs. Adams, also. These are Lieutenant Marlowe's friends, whom I have now met. We were all three of us asked to take tea there one evening, and to dine on another, when the Admiral was also included in the invitation. You will never guess what we talked about with the three sailors – Battles? Storms? Pirates? No, books. It appears they are all great readers while on a voyage, and of novels, too.

"Novels!" cried I.

"Why does that surprise you, madam?" asked the Admiral.

"Well, because . . ." But before I could proceed further he interrupted me.

"Because, I suppose, you imagine that sailors, if they read at all, must always be studying books about their profession?"

I was not to be so easily set-down. "But is there leisure, sir? I admit I know nothing of the Navy. But what about the running of the ship? The sails? The navigation?"

"Ah, madam, that is an error a layman is often apt to fall into. I assure you no man can be on duty twenty-four hours a day, unless he be obliged in the course of a battle."

"Yes, indeed," said Captain Adams, "when one is off watch, there is nothing pleasanter than to retire to the privacy of one's cabin with a book."

"Quite," said the Admiral, "it is a pastime that rests and refreshes one before the next bout with the sea or the enemy. There is a lady writing just now whom I much admire. I wonder if you know her? She has at present published only two novels. I hope she will write many, many more."

"What is her subject, sir?"

"Nothing at all remarkable. That is the charm. Only three or four families in a country village. When I am at sea, I dearly love to escape to that village. That is what is so captivating. It is like going home to England."

"I have not heard of her, you must give me her name, sir," said Captain Adams.

"Her name is not known, sir," replied the Admiral. "Her books are signed 'By a Lady,' merely." (Then to Lieutenant Marlowe) "You should try one, young man, if you have not."

"Yes, sir."

"You do not sound convinced."

"I prefer tales of action, sir, set abroad. *Vathek* and *The Monk* are two of my favourites."

"Ah, you like stirring events in exotic places. Well, well, you are but young. Just wait. Just wait." (Wagging a finger at him.) "When you have a home of your own, you will think very differently."

Lieutenant Marlowe looked somewhat abashed and did not reply. I saw Charlotte watching him, and was much amused by this conversation and all its implications. Alas, these enjoyable social engagements and excursions will soon be drawing to a close. The Admiral has been active on behalf of Lieutenant Marlowe and is hoping to arrange an appointment for him shortly.

But you will be wanting to hear about your Mr. Elton. He is now staying with his friends, but we meet at the Assemblies and in the Pump Room. He is quite indefatigable in his attendance. We see him every time we go, and from what I understand he is present on many other occasions when we are not – getting it all in while he can, I suppose, before he returns to the whist club at Highbury! He has now made other acquaintance, mercifully; so Charlotte and I are left tolerably alone, which pleases her and does not discomfit me.

I strongly suspect he is come to Bath to look for a wife. Why? I ask myself, when all the young women of Highbury are so very willing.

He has a certain ostentatious gallantry that would attach those not nice in their requirements, and has, indeed, since he came, attracted several young women of a more fashionable and worldly appearance than our Charlotte. She is too unaffected and natural for his taste: fortunately so, since he is certainly not to hers.

Soon after that first evening he was taken up by a Mrs. Partridge, not a *lady* according to our notions. She has a friend, a Miss Augusta Hawkins, who is staying with her. We have met them at the Pump-Room, introduced by Mr. Elton. Mr. P. was with us on that occasion, and almost at once this Miss Hawkins started to talk to him about somewhere called Maple Grove, a place of which he had never heard, and did not particularly wish to hear. She raved on about card parties with unbroken packs, separate candles, ices, and even dragged in a barouche-landau! She was evidently wishing to impress him with the importance of her connections, but succeeded in accomplishing exactly the reverse. Mr. Elton appears to be carrying on quite a flirtation with this person. She is, from our observation, a young woman proud, affected and over-dressed.

Why do I trouble to tell you these things? As Mr. P. said to me, paraphrasing *Hamlet* – What is Miss Hawkins to us: Or us to Miss Hawkins? Apparently she and Mrs. Partridge have a large acquaintance here, and go out much into "society," or so we were led to believe by your vicar.

Adieu,

Charlotte

LETTER 25

From Mrs. Goddard to Mrs. Pinkney

Highbury,
26 January 1814

I have not written sooner, my dear Charlotte, because I was uncertain of the direction. I had the idea you might have left Bath already for Sloane Street, and then I thought you had not, yet did not like to address you at the White Hart if you were not there. All this shilly-shallying seems a poor return for your letter, so full of news, particularly about Mr. Elton, which naturally interested me excessively. There seems to be some double-dealing going on. Our perfect Mr. Elton! Who could ever have conceived of it?

Later. My dear Charlotte, I had got no further than that when I was presented with the intelligence that Mr. Elton is to be married! And he has only been gone from Highbury four weeks. It is to the very Miss Hawkins of whom you spoke. I hope your estimation of her is not quite right, because if she is as affected and proud as you say, she will not, as the Vicar's wife, contribute much to the general weal of Highbury.

Such momentous tidings travel fast. As soon as Miss Bates knew, her Patty knew, and she immediately ran over to my Alice and now all my young ladies in the school, as well as Miss Nash, are sunk in gloom. Their hopes dashed! Harriet Smith seems particularly low. A thousand pities she is not safely betrothed to Robert Martin, as she certainly ought to be. The other evening, when she came back from Hartfield, she mentioned that she had met him and his sister shopping at Ford's. Telling me about it, she talked regretfully of never going to the Abbey-Mill Farm again. It is the first time she has spoken to them since he brought the famous parcel and letter in December. I remarked that I trusted she had not had any sort of disagreement with the Martin girls? She said no, to be sure, in such an unhappy flustered way that I had not the heart to pursue the matter.

I had a letter only yesterday from her father with his quarterly remittance. He enclosed more than the usual sum so that she might have some new clothes this spring. I know he would give much to see her well-settled.

January 29th. Oh dear, this letter does go in fits and starts. Alice called me away to settle a dispute between Sarah and Mrs. Wallis, who does extra baking for us on occasion. Sarah, like many a good cook, has a hot temper, and Mrs. Wallis is prone to say a sharp word. It had reached the point where Mrs. Wallis was vowing she would never bake for us again, when Alice, who was in the kitchen at the time, and who, in spite of her queer moods, has the best interests of the school at heart, came running to beg me to intercede.

Thank goodness she did. I found Sarah, arms akimbo, ordering Mrs. Wallis out of her kitchen. I can tell you it took all my powers of tact and persuasion to mollify the one and reverse the decision of the other. They are now quite reconciled. Better friends than ever. Weeping in each others' arms! What a storm in a teacup, and what a toll it does take of one's nerves. I could not do without either of these good women, and the children would be desolate if we were no longer to have Mrs. Wallis's currant buns on Wednesdays. But there! You are not interested in affairs of the kitchen, only of the heart.

What other news can I relate of this busy little place? Oh yes, Miss Fairfax has arrived. At least *her* heart seems whole. She is her usual refined, reserved self that I have known these many years. She does not change, except to become if anything more elegant. She appears quite content to be at her grandmother's, which is rather wonderful when you consider the sad contrast between the Bateses very small rooms and the comfortable style of living she is accustomed to in her home at Colonel Campbell's. In particular, she must feel the want of a pianoforte.

I have invited her to the school, have told her that she is welcome to practise on any of our instruments. She did venture once. The third day she was here. But I fear our battered old spinets, hammered on by generations of children at their scales are not conducive to her superior notions of music making. And *that* is to say nothing of the noise and chatter – what *you* would call pandemonium, and *I* would call cheerful bustle – of the girls in the passage. Although she thanked me most graciously, I am sure she will not be back.

Your affectionate sister,
M. Goddard

LETTER 26

From Mrs. Pinkney to Mrs. Goddard

Sloane Street
London
7 February 1814

My dear Mary,

I should have written to you before, but since I could write nothing that was not a *complaint*, which I know you do not care for, I did not write at all.

Your news of Mr. Elton and Miss Hawkins was no great surprise. As I observed them at the Assemblies she very evidently wanting to fix him, and he seemed more than ready for any eligible young woman likely to accept his proposals.

The fact that he did not choose one of the young ladies at Highbury more than ever convinces me that he made Miss Woodhouse an offer, and was refused. Pride would then preclude him selecting another from the same confined circle.

We are now back in London, as you can see.

Admiral Seymour having secured an appointment for Lieutenant Marlowe to Portsmouth, (with a few tears shed by Charlotte) and himself deciding to quit the place, our happy little party was quite broken-up, so Mr. P. decided there was nothing to detain us longer in Bath.

We were determined we would not go until we could get all four seats together inside the coach, and as not so many people are travelling at this season, within a few days we were successful. This time our journey was safely accomplished. Charlotte is now imprisoned (her word) back at that school with nothing to do, I conclude, but read to the younger ones and pine for the navy.

The other day she asked me in a most conscious manner if I knew the navy toast: to, "The wind that blows, The ship that goes, And the lass that loves a sailor." I said I had not heard it before, and how charming I thought it. So she loves him, evidently! It does not surprise me.

I, myself, am in a very melancholy mood now we are back in Sloane Street. The house is dark and gloomy as ever and the cares of housekeeping are again upon me. Mr. P. has once more retreated to his study, and I miss my fresh young companion whom I now see only for an hour or so when she can get away. After the cheerful noise and goings on at the White Hart, the lively chatter of young Charlotte and our evening visits to the play or the Assembly, I find the quiet and solitude of this house depressing beyond words. Yes, Mary, I know exactly what you will say, but such a style of living decidedly does not suit me.

Mr. P. has lost his other friend and companion of the chess board. The yellow clergyman has gone on a visit to Wales of some weeks. He, therefore, has nothing to do and is in a depressed state also. While young Charlotte and the Admiral were with us, we seemed to have plenty to talk about; now, we have nothing, and Mr. P., who was amiable and conversible in Bath, has sunk into silence again. I have once more offered to learn chess, but he declines to teach me. He is probably right. It would bore me to death. I am sure I would not have the patience for it.

As for your Harriet, it seems to me she is too vacillating to deserve Robert Martin. But I know your wishes in this matter, so I will say no more, except to sign myself,

Ever your affectionate sister,
Charlotte

LETTER 27

From Mrs. Goddard to Mrs. Pinkney

Highbury,
12 February 1814

My dear Charlotte,

The girls are at their lessons, the maids at their work, I have done my accounts, and am free to write to you.

You do sound despondent. I am sorry, but I am even sorrier for your husband. Since you say you know what my advice would be, pray imagine it said and act upon it. You were writing so cheerfully from Bath, I had hopes that you were managing better. If one is not happy at home, one is indeed to be pitied, for that is where one must inevitably be.

Well, Mr. Elton has come and gone. He was one week here before leaving for his wedding. He did indeed look quite flushed with success, as he strolled – goodness me, I nearly wrote *strutted* about the town: allowable in a would-be bridegroom, I daresay. The trunk you saw at the White Hart was also seen by Harriet in the butcher's waggon on its way to the coach. Unpacked and re-packed, I conjecture, with new clothes for his wedding. Alas, that you are no longer in Bath to tell us all about it, as, knowing you, you would have been bound to have found out some intelligence in the matter.

Until he returns with his bride, when I presume I shall have something of more sensational interest to report, you must be content with the usual sort of Highbury news.

Three days ago Elizabeth Martin called here. Harriet was out, but she left her a note. And yesterday, actually the day Mr. Elton departed for Bath, Miss Woodhouse, quite on the spur of the moment, it seems, drove Harriet in the carriage to the farm

94

and put her down at the door! Do you suppose her conscience could have got the better of her? I had sent my remembrances to Mrs. Martin, and when Harriet returned I asked how she did, and the girls, and what news there was of the family in general. Harriet blushed and said she hardly knew how to answer my questions as she was only there fifteen minutes. Miss Woodhouse had come back in the carriage to pick her up and must not be kept waiting.

"Fifteen minutes!" cried I. "Fifteen minutes given to people with whom you were glad last summer to spend six weeks. Mrs. Martin must have thought that very extraordinary."

Harriet hung her head and had the grace to look ashamed. "Very true. To be sure. Yes."

She seemed close to tears, so I said no more. Certainly not much of friendship could be re-established in a quarter of an hour; yet relations have not been entirely broken off and I must cling to that and not lose all hope for the foolish girl.

Oh, how could I forget. We have a novelty in Highbury. Mr. Elton has left, but Mr. Frank Churchill has come. He has actually arrived at last. I first saw him in the High Street, the day before yesterday, walking with his father. He is an exceedingly handsome and agreeable young man; Mr. Weston was fairly beaming with pride as he introduced me. Mr. Churchill at once said he had often heard of my school, and what an excellent reputation it had far afield from Highbury. Of course I was gratified, even if I took it as mere flattery. He knows how to please, evidently.

They had been to call at Hartfield, and while Mr. Weston was at that very moment going into the Crown about his hay, his son was intending, meantime, to visit the Bateses. He had been slightly acquainted with Miss Fairfax at Weymouth when she was visiting there with the Campbells.

All this was very right, proper and as it should be; so I was all the more shocked to learn that *today*, after being here just over forty-eight hours, Frank Churchill has gone off to London to have his hair cut!

I suppose it is the school mistress in me, but I cannot say I approve. Such a want of consideration for his father and Mrs.

Weston. Such extravagance. I understand through my Alice, who is friendly with the Westons' Hannah, daughter of Mr. Woodhouse's James, that he returned in very good spirits, as if he had accomplished something miraculous in town rather than a visit to the barber, merely.

Mrs. Weston, whom I met earlier today at Ford's, takes it very well, only saying that young people will have their little whims. She is a good woman, I never heard her speaking ill of anybody, or at least she always finds an extenuating circumstance.

Pray write, dear Charlotte, and assure me that you are feeling more cheerful. I am concerned for you and Mr. Pinkney.

Ever your aff. sister,
M. Goddard

P.S. A note has just come from Mr. Woodhouse, brought round by James, inviting me to dine at Hartfield on Tuesday. Miss Woodhouse is to dine at the Coles'.

LETTER 28

From Mrs. Pinkney to Mrs. Goddard

Sloane Street
14 February 1814

My dear Mary,

I am answering your letter immediately having nothing else to do and wanting someone to talk to.

So Frank Churchill has deigned to honour Highbury at last. I shall be interested to hear how his visit goes on, and whose heart he catches. If he is as handsome as you say, and there is such a dearth of eligible young men in Highbury, perhaps your Harriet and Miss Woodhouse may become rivals for his hand. Would that not be diverting?

As for his riding to London to get his hair cut, words fail me. The sixteen miles between Highbury and London might as well be sixteen hundred as far as I am concerned. Oh, the evils of being a dependent woman! Why must we rely on *men*?

It seems, however, that the majority of us cannot do without them. Every day Charlotte calls here and she has but one subject of conversation – Lieutenant Marlowe. She is forever wondering what he must be doing *now*, what he is reading, who he is with, and recalling with solicitude things he said and incidents that occurred when we were together in Bath. It does get a little tedious, but I try to listen with as much sympathy as I can muster, remembering what it was like, so long ago when one was young and in love, to be separated from one's beloved. I had a letter from the young gentleman soon after we arrived back in town, ostensibly to thank me for including him in our various parties to the theatre, etc. He was at some pains to describe his present activities at Portsmouth – he is intermittently at sea, chasing smugglers, and asked to be remembered to Charlotte. I replied, as no doubt he hoped I would, giving him all news of *her*, how Madame Dubois has put her to teaching the little ones, because she is not paying full fees, (not that I told him *that*) ending with sending her remembrances. What a contrivance!

Mr. Wingfield has just called, and Mr. P., happening to be in the parlour with me when he arrived, (a most unusual circumstance), Mr. W. was able to speak to both of us at once. Although not shining in social conversation, when it comes to matters of health he has a disconcerting knack of being able to elicit more information than I, for one, intended to give. He remarked that we did not seem in such good spirits as when we had first returned from Bath, and he did not wish to see a recurrence of Mr. P.'s gout.

"No more do I, sir," said Mr. P.

"Very well, then, sir," said Mr. W., "I shall give you an invaluable prescription."

Of course I expected some sort of tablet or powder for Mr. P. to swallow. But, no. To my astonishment Mr. W proceeded to give us the following instructions. Mr. P. is to continue modest eating and drinking habits, is not to sit cooped up inside, hunched over the chess board, *and*, he is to walk for one hour daily. Furthermore, if you please, Mr. W. as good as ordered *me* to go with him! "For health and for companionship," was the actual edict. Can you believe it? Since Mr. P. thinks the world of Mr. W. and his advice, we are to follow it. So one hour a day I shall be alone in company with my husband. Heaven knows what we will talk about.

Adieu,

Charlotte

LETTER 29

From Mrs. Goddard to Mrs. Pinkney

Highbury,
15 February 1814

Mr. Wingfield does seem to have given you most unusual instructions, my dear Charlotte. But they sound extremely sagacious. I hope you are following them faithfully. Surely it should not be such a penance to spend one hour a day with one's own husband? The simple regimen prescribed, I imagine cannot fail of being beneficial. Perhaps, in the interests of health, Mr. Pinkney may even be persuaded to attempt a basin of gruel. – dear Mr. Woodhouse's favourite late evening dish.

I am answering yours immediately because I have a bit of news which, although it would be nothing in London where no doubt instruments are delivered daily, has us all agog here in Highbury. Besides, there is another mystery for you to solve.

Yesterday, an anonymous person sent Miss Fairfax a pianoforte. It came from Broadwood's by waggon in the morning. I say "anonymous," but it is generally thought to be from Colonel Campbell – though his most recent letter did not mention any such impending gift. It is, in fact, a complete and total surprise.

The Bateses' staircase being very narrow with a turn and an awkward step, the pianoforte could not be got up that way; a casement window upstairs had to be removed, the legs taken off and the instrument hauled up with a block and tackle. I actually heard the commotion from within the school, and walked out to see for myself what was happening. You will not be surprised to learn that I found quite a crowd had gathered in the High Street, and for a time all passage was restricted. The wagoneers were very clever and capable, and are evidently used to such things. Miss Bates was outside, talking and admiring, getting in the way and generally obstructing progress. It was from her that I learned they could only suppose the gift to come from Colonel Campbell. Well, you can imagine how it has set us all talking!

Tonight there is to be a large dinner party at the Coles', who are entertaining in their new-built dining parlour for the first time. To keep Mr. Woodhouse company in his daughter's absence, Mrs. Bates has also been summoned to dine with me at Hartfield. I am sure there will be a good dinner. The question is: will we be allowed to eat it?

Yours affectionately,
M. Goddard

LETTER 30

From Mrs. Pinkney to Mrs. Goddard

Sloane Street
London
17 February 1814

Really, dear Mary, the answer is as plain as the nose on your face.

Did you not observe the date of your own letter? February the 15th and you spoke of "yesterday." The day on which the pianoforte was delivered was St. Valentine's Day. It is the gift of an impetuous young man, I'll warrant you.

In the course of our walk I mentioned the matter to Mr. P. and he declares that you can depend upon it that no man of sense, no mature man of judgement, no Colonel Campbell, would send without warning such an article as to cause so much inconvenience to the Bateses. If their quarters are as confined as you say, it must have been with considerable difficulty that they even found space to accommodate the instrument. But who the person can be? that is another question. You must send me more information when you have it. When I facetiously wrote in October that I wished you had some mystery at Highbury for me to exercise my wits about, little did I think you would be able to supply so many. You know how I relish these puzzles, and you seem to have puzzles aplenty in Highbury.

Our weather here has continued damp and dirty with frost in the mornings. Still Mr. P. and I persevere with our instructions. I put on my half-boots, and we sally forth together. We usually leave the house about noon, and then look forward to a visit from Charlotte when we return. I must concede, I suppose, that we are both benefitting from this enforced exercise. Mr. P. is more cheerful, and I have lost some of the extra flesh I put on while we were in Bath.

There is much to be observed in the streets of London, which furnishes subjects for conversation as we march along, for Mr. Wingfield has decreed that we must walk briskly and not dawdle or stroll. Although I used to think that I enjoyed walking in the country when I lived in Yorkshire, there is more variety in town.

Sometimes we go to the circulating library. This morning I did try to obtain a book by that lady the Admiral was telling us about, but with no success; so I took *Belinda* instead, and Mr. P. got *An essay on Naval Tactics*, of which, he tells me, Nelson is said to have expressed his approbation. Mr. P.'s conversations with the sailors we met at Bath have quite whetted his interest in naval subjects. I am delighted he should have something else to think about besides chess, which I am happy to say he has not played in this long while. I quite dread the return of his friend from Wales, as I am afraid he may shut himself up in his room again, which is not good for anything, and does not make for sociability.

Here is Charlotte come.

Affectionately,
C. Pinkney

P.S. Why were you not invited to the Coles' party? Is she not a friend of yours? And as to our eating gruel. Mr. Pinkney says, certainly not! Not under any circumstances!

LETTER 31

From Mrs. Goddard to Mrs. Pinkney

Highbury,
19 February 1814

How clever you are, dear Charlotte. St. Valentine's Day, of course! Well, I shall be upon the watch, but I doubt it is possible, certainly for me, and perhaps not even for you, to discover who this lover is.

Yes, to be sure Mrs. Cole is a friend to me, as indeed she is to everyone in Highbury; a very unpretentious, good-hearted woman, who, in spite of her husband's ever-increasing wealth, thinks little of her own importance. There is no reason why she should ask me, a widow, a mistress of a school, to her dinner party. What could I contribute of interest to the conversation? Miss Bates no doubt furnishes enough trivialities for both of us. Oh dear, that just slipped out. How very unkind! I am quite ashamed of myself. She is such a good soul, and probably the most popular woman in Highbury. It is not at all surprising that she should be asked to the Coles', especially as her niece is to be there.

I passed a pleasant evening at Hartfield, notwithstanding. I walked over to the Bateses, and James called for Mrs. Bates and me promptly at half past three and at four we sat down to an excellent dinner. We had pease soup, fried Hartfield pork steaks without the smallest grease, and baked apples and cream. Fortunately Mr. Woodhouse for once considered the meal to be thoroughly wholesome and we were permitted to eat everything. Dear old Mrs. Bates is very fond of eating. Poor old lady, she does not dine near so well at home. After dinner Miss Woodhouse came and sat with us a few minutes before leaving for the Coles'. She looked very handsome and kindly cut us large slices of cake and filled our glasses with wine, fearful we had not had enough, no doubt.

We three old people played piquet; but the good dinner she had consumed was almost too much for Mrs. Bates. She kept nodding off in her chair. I was obliged to raise my voice rather loudly whenever it was her turn to play. Mr. Woodhouse hardly noticed, he kept talking of his daughter and conjecturing every moment how she was faring; afraid she might be over-tired: afraid she might catch cold; afraid her maid would not wait up for her, then ringing for the butler, yet again, to make sure that this had been arranged. I believe this is the first time he has ever been alone without her of an evening. It is almost pitiable to see how much he depends on her, and it is greatly to her credit, I think – as a young person – how very kind and patient she always is with him.

The carriage took us home after tea, which was earlier than the Coles' party broke up. James and his horses had a busy night trotting about Highbury.

They brought Harriet home in due course. I sat up and waited for her. She gave me a glowing account; Miss Fairfax and Miss Woodhouse played and sang, Miss Fairfax in Italian which impressed my artless little girl. No Italian taught in this school! Frank Churchill also sang very delightfully, and afterward there was dancing – the furniture being pushed back, and kind Mrs. Weston playing country dances for the young people on Mrs. Coles' new grand pianoforte. Harriet said that Frank Churchill quite singled out Miss Woodhouse in his attentions. Well, *there* is a match which I am sure the Westons would be delighted to see take place, and heaven knows he is rich enough and handsome enough to deserve her. She may declare she will never marry, but she must be tempted by such a very charming young man.

Harriet has evidently some lingering regrets over the Martins. She was gossiping this morning with Miss Nash about the Cox girls. Robert Martin dined there recently and she was troubled by the notion that Anne Cox might fancy him. And so she might! As any sensible, unpretending girl would do.

Later. I had hoped to post this this morning, but various domestic cares prevented me from folding and sealing it, and now I have something more to add about the mystery of the pianoforte that I neglected to mention before.

Harriet told me that the morning after the Coles' party she and Miss Woodhouse met Mrs. Weston and Frank Churchill at Ford's, and were persuaded to go along to the Bateses to hear the new instrument. Apparently a set of Irish songs had been sent with it. While they were all together and Miss Fairfax was about to sit down to play, Frank Churchill commented on this to her, "Very thoughtful of Colonel Campbell, was not it?"

Harriet is never very quick, but she did notice that Miss Fairfax looked very conscious and that Mr. Churchill made quite a pointed little speech to her, saying, "only true affection could have prompted" including music. She said Miss Fairfax quite flushed at the remark. Harriet took this to mean the affection of Colonel Campbell, and thinking of her own situation, no doubt, observed how fortunate Miss Fairfax was in having been – so to speak – adopted by such a very kind man.

But you and I think we know better, do we not? But who is it? Was Frank Churchill hinting at a particular person? Or was it just a comment, tossed off, that happened to hit the mark?

Yours ever,

M. Goddard

P.S. Rather ironic. The music master has just come to see me complaining about the condition of the third spinet. He says it is falling to pieces and he insists that it be replaced before the start of the next school year. But where am I to find such a thing in Highbury? I do not have the wherewithal to order an instrument sent down from Broadwood's as Miss Fairfax's was.

LETTER 32

From Mrs. Pinkney to Mrs. Goddard

Sloane Street
London
21 February 1814

My dear Mary,

First Harriet, then Jane Fairfax and now my Charlotte! Oh, these girls! How their affairs of the heart touch us all! Even me and Mr. Pinkney.

The reason I concluded my last so abruptly was that a few days previously a letter had arrived here addressed to Charlotte. I thought I recognized the hand, and deduced the writer would hardly have sent it care of myself without some purpose. I therefore locked it away in my writing desk instead of having Betty take it over to the school. As Charlotte had missed calling, being kept in by that dreadful woman to teach the little ones, I had had the letter several days when she arrived, just as I was writing to you.

"Good morning, my dear," said I, as soon as she entered the room. "I am glad you are come, for I have something very particular here for you."

"What can it be, madam?"

"A letter!" And I produced it with a flourish.

She took it with a little squeak of joy and surprise. Of course I begged her not to stand upon ceremony. She thanked me and withdrew to the window where I watched her eagerly breaking open the seal.

I am sure you have guessed the identity of her correspondent. When she had finished reading, she looked up and with some hesitation addressed me thus,

"Mrs. Pinkney, you are my only friend in the world" – then correcting herself – "*almost* my only friend, and I want to ask your advice."

"Pray do," I said, knowing pretty well what was coming.

"This letter is from Lieutenant Marlowe," she announced in a happy fearful tone.

"No!" Then, unable to resist teasing her a little, "is he well?"

"Er . . . yes . . . very well." And there she stopped.

"Has he been often at sea?"

"I am not sure, madam. Yes, I think he has."

I knew I should bait her no longer, so I said, "Please continue, what was it you wished to ask me?"

"He wants me to write to him." She hesitated again. "I know it's wrong . . ."

"I am sure you are aware, child," said I as pompously as possible, "that it is considered extremely improper to correspond with a man unless you are engaged to him?"

She looked perturbed. "Yes, but . . ."

"You are not engaged to him?"

"No . . . er . . . not exactly."

"Exactly," said I, pausing, and looking her full in the face. "But by all means I would advise you to do so."

"Oh, madam," she cried, all joy and confusion, "that's not what I expected you to say."

"No doubt it is not. But I am not one to observe convention for convention's sake, especially when it does no harm to anyone. If ever you were to marry, your knowledge of each other will be much improved by an exchange of letters."

"Very true, yes, madam."

"Of course," I said smiling, "you might argue that it is better *not* to know too much about the person with whom you are to spend your life."

She looked as if she did not understand this remark. So I

simply said, "Charlotte, if you were my own daughter, I would still give you this advice. Write to him, by all means."

"Oh, thank you, m'am," she cried, her face radiant. "It can't be so very wrong can it? He's alone and I'm alone, and I do like him so very much."

"Well," I said, doing my best to keep my countenance, "no doubt it is, as you say. I presume you do not want letters sent to the school, I shall ask Mr. Pinkney if you may use this address."

The letter had been posted on St. Valentine's Day. The young man was missing her so much, he could restrain himself no longer. This is what I conveyed to Mr. P., when I broached the subject on our walk.

"I hope I can make you understand her situation," I said to him, "because you probably do not know what it is like to be young and desperately in love."

"What makes you think so, madam?"

"I beg your pardon," said I, astonished.

"When I was not much older than Lieutenant Marlowe I was deeply attached to a young woman. Our wedding was arranged and all the preparations made."

I hardly knew what to say, remembering only too clearly the time he had agreed that a true love could never be supplanted. With shame I recalled our conversation about *Evelina*, how I had run out of the room and how distressed he had been. I murmured something sympathetic, and we walked the next few steps in silence. For a moment I feared he might say no more. Then, with a sigh, he told me in a low voice that Fanny had died of a putrid fever a week before their wedding, and that he had been inconsolable.

"So that is why you shut yourself up at Cambridge and never married?"

He nodded, his heart seemed to be too full to speak.

I put my arm through his. "I am very sorry, Mr. Pinkney. I did not mean to give you pain."

"Madam," said he. "I do not believe that we understand each other as well as we might."

Dear Mary, I blush to write these words. So busy have I been puzzling out the dilemmas of Highbury and occupying myself with Charlotte's affairs, that I have given little thought to my own husband. Poor Mr. P. looked so desolate when he told me this sad tale of his lost love, that my heart quite went out to him. Suddenly I saw our situation as you have often tried to point it out to me, not from my own selfish perspective, but from his. He had taken a wife into his household and what felicity was she bringing him?

While I was musing on these things, and before I could bring myself to reply, he spoke again.

"I feel I have disappointed you," he said, looking at me earnestly. "What ought I to have done? Remember, I never have been married before; I have always lived among men."

I was taken aback by this direct question. "You must not reproach yourself, sir," I said. "You have been very generous both to me and to young Charlotte. We all enjoyed ourselves at Bath."

"Yes. But now we are at home that enjoyment has ceased."

This was too true to be contradicted, yet still I lacked courage to proceed. How could I bring myself to tell him my true feelings? After a silence it seemed neither of us was willing to break, he said,

"What was it you wanted to tell me about young Charlotte?"

"Mr. Pinkney," said I, deciding that now was the moment, a moment that might never occur again. "Will you answer me a question?"

"If I can, of course, madam."

"Why did you ask me to marry you?"

"I beg your pardon?"

"Was it to replace Mrs. Wilson?"

"Certainly not. Whatever gave you such a notion?"

I was conscious that he was staring at me in amazement.

"I was under that impression," I said. "Was I wrong?"

"Very wrong. I married you because I thought I should like you to be my wife. I had been too long alone. When my uncle died and left me a sufficient income, I determined to leave Cambridge and to change my way of living entirely. You had the advantage of being the widow of my friend. Furthermore, I was aware that, with respect, Grenville had never been – well, entirely *responsible* when it came to financial matters, and I saw that you were, frankly, in need of a husband."

"Really, sir?" I said, both bemused and touched.

"I had come to realize that I did not wish to end my life without ever having been married. I wanted a companion. Your reputation, as I heard it from your husband, was that you were lively, a women of spirit. I thought we would be cheerful together."

This was altogether nearly too much for me. *Cheerful* is what we never have been. The poor man! It seemed that none of his hopes had been realized in this marriage. In my consternation, all I could think of saying was, "And I have disappointed *you*!" Thus I found myself echoing the very words he had used to me, and I recalled how oppressed I had been when first I arrived in his dark, gloomy house where I had no acquaintance and felt so dreadfully alone. "How could I be lively," I continued, "when you left me by myself for hours on end, while you shut yourself up in your room with your chess board and that horrible old man?"

"I was disheartened," said he, "and reluctant to intrude upon your privacy. I believed that you regretted our marriage, and I did not know what to do or say, I am not adept at the arts necessary to please a woman."

"They are not very difficult," I said attempting a smile. "Perhaps I could teach you?"

"Perhaps you could, madam. I believe we have each misunderstood the other. What should we do? Pray speak freely."

I took a deep breath. "I wish you would not spend so much time in your study."

"Indeed, I would be extremely glad not to do so. I am heartily sick of the chess board and Fowler's crowing cackle whenever he wins."

I was delighted to hear this, "Thank goodness."

"I would not stay there," he continued, "if I felt you cared for my company."

"I am sure I could learn to care for it very much, if I ever had any of it. How comfortable we were together at Bath."

"Yes," he agreed, "we were."

"At Bath," I said, "we had much enjoyment and good conversation. Here in town, we see no one, and in consequence we have nothing to say. If I am to be lively I cannot do with seeing nobody. Let us go out more."

He bowed. "You wish me to accompany you?"

"Of course. I cannot go alone. Besides, you are my husband."

"I have been at the university all my life," said he.

"That is no reason," said I, "to stay at home. It is time for a change."

"It will, indeed, for me be a very great change."

"But that is something you began when you left Cambridge and took a wife."

"True," he said.

"You have been used to teach, now it is time to learn."

"If you say so," (actually smiling).

"Oh, I do say so," I cried, quite struck at my own boldness; but I saw that our future happiness depended on me concealing nothing of what I had been thinking. "Then there is also the house."

"The house?"

"It is too dark. It affects my spirits, and I believe yours also."

"So you wish me to change my house, as well as my way of living? Is that all, madam?"

I smiled. "It will do for now."

"Oh, it will, will it?"

"The penalty for taking a lively wife, sir?"

He looked at me quizzically, then he laughed and pressed my arm. "I shall see what I can do."

Dear Mary, you can imagine my feelings; after all this time to find that inside my sober-seeming, scholarly-appearing husband there actually existed a human being with a sense of humour. What a benefaction! I hope I have not overstepped the bounds of propriety in telling you these things. But knowing your concern and remembering the advice you have often given me, I felt you would be very much interested. I cannot tell you how my spirits have been uplifted since this conversation, and Mr. Pinkney is actually smiling as he goes about the house.

Needless to say, he made no difficulty about Charlotte. He is willing to do anything to oblige me, it seems, and has generously offered to pay for the letters. So when she called the next day, I was able to tell her that she might use our address as a *poste restante*.

I need not describe her joy. They are very young, and cannot be engaged, I suppose, because if he should want to marry he will have to get his captain's permission, which I am sure would not be forthcoming yet awhile even if the attachment should last so long. I don't know what will come of the affair, but no harm, I'll be bound.

But is it not curious that her little romance with Lieutenant Marlowe should indirectly be the means of effecting this *eclaircissement* between Mr. Pinkney and myself?

And speaking of romance – so you consider that Frank Churchill is rich enough and handsome enough to make a match with Emma Woodhouse, do you? But have you thought what is to be done with her father? You mention that when she went to the Coles' party, she was for the first time leaving him alone for the evening. Even if she should wish to, how can she possibly marry? From what you say, I cannot imagine that Mr. Woodhouse will ever be prevailed upon either to leave Hartfield or to sanction her doing so.

Your newly-enlightened and happy sister,
Charlotte

P.S. I must chide you for referring to yourself as one of the 'old people.' At your age, it is absurd to be thus aligning yourself with Mrs. Bates.

LETTER 33

From Mrs. Goddard to Mrs. Pinkney

Highbury,
23 February 1814

Nothing could have given me greater satisfaction, my dear, dear Charlotte, than your most recent letter. Somehow I always felt that good sense and right feeling would overcome your difficulties in the end.

Extraordinary that they should have arisen from a misapprehension on both sides. *He* believing you had regretted your decision to marry him and *you* assuming that he only wanted a housekeeper. I hope you will now be a real wife to him and find your happiness together. Oh dear, am I lecturing again? A hazard of my occupation, I fear.

As for Charlotte and Lieutenant Marlowe, although it is certainly extremely unconventional, since there is nobody else to be affected by their writing to each other, I see no harm in condoning the correspondence. She has little enough of this world's joys. How fortunate that she should have found a soul mate, if that is what he is, or proves to be.

Young people are indeed a source of interest to those "old folk" like ourselves who merely stand on the side and watch.

As for your chiding me for calling myself old, I devoutly hope I will not be considered so by Mr. and Mrs. Weston, because Harriet informs me that they are planning a ball at the Crown; in honour of Frank Churchill, I presume. Now an invitation to *that* I should dearly love to receive.

It is years since we had a ball at Highbury. But I suppose one might have foretold that when two such novelties as Frank Churchill and Jane Fairfax are introduced into our confined

111

society changes are bound to occur. It would give me the greatest pleasure to sit nicely dressed by the fire, drink wine, and observe the young people dancing. But if I am required to stay with Mr. Woodhouse I shall go without a murmur, except to you, dear Charlotte.

Yours aff:ly.
M. G.

P.S. The ball is cancelled. So much for false hopes. Our young people will be desolate. I have just heard that Frank Churchill has been sent for and was obliged to leave Highbury yesterday. Mrs. Churchill is ill – or says she is – again.

LETTER 34

From Mrs. Pinkney to Mrs. Goddard

Sloane Street
4 March 1814

My dear Mary,

What a merry dance that wretched woman does lead those connected with her! I am sorry her supposed illness should be the cause of your losing your ball. It would have been such a charming diversion for you.

Yes, I knew you would be pleased to hear what I had to relate concerning Mr. P. and myself. We continue our walks in a spirit of harmony and friendship not present before. Mr. P. has undertaken my London education. Every day we visit a different sight. Yesterday we went to look at No. 8 Russell Street where Boswell met Johnson at Davies' shop. Mr. P. amused me very much by recalling the set-down the doctor had given Boswell on the occasion. Tomorrow we are to go to St. Paul's and watch the

College Youths practise ringing the bells. It is as complicated as chess, Mr. P. declares. He says he would be happy to explain to me the art of change ringing, only doubts I would be interested in the mathematical procedures it entails.

And lest you think our conversation is usually about intellectual matters, let me asure you it is not. I believe we are now each anxious to make the best possible impression on the other. I am pleased to tell you that Mr. P. is actually becoming a most agreeable husband. I am sure you remember me envying Miss Taylor her happiness on her marriage, I think I may say that I am in a fair way to being happy myself.

Furthermore, I have discovered that unlike most men he loves a gossip, a relic of his old Cambridge days, I imagine. All the varieties of character to be found in people, both those we know, and those we do not know, amuse him. It is a subject on which we have much entertaining discourse; the good people of Highbury figuring largely, you may be sure.

I have regaled him with everything I can about the place. His interest is piqued, particularly over the incident of Miss Fairfax's pianoforte. He is applying his excellent chess brain to the question. With such meagre clues as you have given me, and without being present, himself, to observe the demeanour of the actual persons, how it is possible to arrive at any solution I cannot conceive.

Charlotte continues in a state of bliss, eagerly rushing over here to collect her letters. She hears astonishingly often from the gallant sailor, except when he is at sea and cannot write. He is now about to go on convoy duty, to combat the ravages of the American privateers which are infesting the Channel and very successfully blocking our trade. She said Lieutenant Marlowe told her that often there are Americans sailing in our ships and Englishmen in American ships: sometimes brother is fighting brother. What times we live in!

Adieu,

C. P.

LETTER 35

From Mrs. Goddard to Mrs. Pinkney

Highbury,
11 March 1814

My dear Charlotte,

I am delighted that all is going along so well between you and Mr. Pinkney and that the affairs of Highbury amuse you both. Now here is more for your delectation.

Mr. and Mrs. Elton have come. Miss Hawkins, that was, has burst upon the scene. She first appeared yesterday at church, and I fear very little attention was paid to the service in consequence. She occupied the vicarage pew, poor old Mrs. Bates has been relegated to a less-favoured spot. She is certainly extremely elegant – in her dress at least – perhaps too much so for a place such as this. But I am severe. She is, after all, a bride. When the service was over there was a crowd about Mr. and Mrs. Elton at the door. Miss Nash and I judged it best to escort our forty young ladies back for their Sunday cold meat. I determined to pay my respects on another occasion.

Well, I wish Mr. Pinkney joy of discovering who Miss Fairfax's lover is. It is certainly diverting to speculate. I need some diversion myself, at present. I am having more difficulty with my maid Alice. I have always been very fond of her, and cannot understand what has wrought this change. If matters do not improve, I shall have to consider sending her away, which would grieve me very much.

Wednesday. Having no more than the above to say, I thought I would keep my letter open until I could report on Mrs. Elton, about whom I feel sure you would like to hear.

We have all been calling on her. Harriet and Miss Woodhouse were among the first. Harriet had very little to tell on the subject, she is not usually so reticent. It appeared to give her positive pain to visit the Vicarage, a place she so minutely and enthusiastically described to me on the occasion of the bootlace incident only three months ago.

I went alone to pay my visit. The Vicarage has been considerably smartened up since the good Bateses lived there. A profusion of pictures, ornaments and the famous yellow curtains, which look better than one would expect. Mr. Elton was out and I had the lady to myself. She plied me with questions – quite beyond what was civil. Did I know who were Mrs. Weston's parents? How had Mr. Cole made his fortune? Why had Mr. Knightley – quite the gentleman! – never married? Where did the girls in my school chiefly come from? She imagined the lower ranks of society, people of quality being more inclined to educate their daughters in town or with a governess; her sister, Mrs. Suckling, of Maple Grove (*there* is that place she spoke to you about) would never dream of sending *her* girls from home.

Her presumption extended to supposing I had trouble keeping teachers in so small a place. It was with difficulty that I maintained my composure as I informed her that Miss Nash, Miss Prince and Miss Richardson had all been with me for several years. Mrs. Elton *then* had the insolence to suggest that *that* no doubt was because they had not been able to "catch a husband"! Those were her very words, dear Charlotte.

She then went on to say that she understood there was one female at least in my school who had had the highest hopes of ensnaring Mr. Elton. With an affected laugh she declared that her "caro sposo" was not to be so easily trapped.

You can imagine my utter astonishment. It appears Mr. Elton must have told her about poor little Harriet. No wonder Harriet did not relish calling at the Vicarage, as I can assure you, after that last example of ill-breeding, no more did I.

It cost me an effort, but I remained resolutely civil while vowing I would not soon be visiting there again.

Yours in righteous indignation,
Mary

.LETTER 36

From Mrs. Pinkney to Mrs. Goddard

Sloane Street
14 March 1814

Mrs. Elton! Insufferable woman! A conclusion I had already formed at Bath. Little did I imagine when I first saw her there that she would fetch up at Highbury. A place *I* am still waiting to visit.

Poor little Harriet! How vile of Mr. Elton to betray her. And surely the child had very good reason for believing herself the one preferred?

The charade, offered as it was as a contribution to her book, certainly *appeared* to be meant for Harriet. Yet, as Mr. P. points out, if it had been, since Mr. Elton was evidently bent on marriage, it is she who would now be mistress of the vicarage. Mrs. Elton can only have heard these details, or at least what he chose to tell her, from her own unpleasant *caro sposo*.

But how could he be aware that Harriet expected him to make her an offer? *We* know how low she was when the news came of his going to Bath, and then, again, on his subsequent engagement. But he could not know these things.

Mr. P. and I are now completely convinced that he wanted to marry Emma Woodhouse, while *she* wanted him to marry Harriet. It seems pretty clear that she was also deluded into thinking Harriet was his object. Some of this must have come out in her refusal of him. Imagine the scene. His making her an offer when she thought he was after her friend! Whatever did she say? Mr. P. and I are persuaded from our observation of him at Bath that Mr. Elton has a very good opinion of himself. You, yourself, said in one of your letters that you did not know who in Highbury he would consider worthy to be his consort. Certainly not Harriet Smith.

If we are correct, it would account for his sudden departure for Bath. Having made an offer – as we suppose – to Miss Woodhouse – and been refused – how could he possibly make do with a second choice in a place the size of Highbury? It would also explain Miss Woodhouse's coming round to the school after Christmas, her talking to Harriet and Harriet's subsequent tears. Poor Emma Woodhouse! I remember your telling me that she was instrumental in making the match between Miss Taylor and Mr. Weston. I suppose she thought she could make another. So, having discouraged Harriet from marrying the completely suitable Robert Martin, and encouraged her to be in love with the hopelessly unsuitable Mr. Elton, she was then obliged to undertake the unpleasant office of informing her friend that *she* was the one to whom the offer had been made.

All speculation, my dear Mary, but we feel confident we have come pretty close to the truth.

I remain, dear Mary, your affectionate sister, the solver of mysteries,

Charlotte

LETTER 37

From Mrs. Goddard to Mrs. Pinkney

Highbury,
9 April 1814

I have been very busy about the chicken pox, my dear Charlotte, and have been remiss about writing. Spring cleaning will be upon us next.

Well! You may not know where Lake Erie is, but your conjectures about Miss Woodhouse and Mr. Elton are most convincing. We may never discover what really happened, but certainly Harriet seems determined to avoid Mr. Elton at all costs.

Today she declined an invitation to dine later this week at Hartfield: a party to honour the bridal couple. I have never known Harriet refuse an invitation from Miss Woodhouse before. A contrast, indeed, from her bitter tears when she was unable to go to the Westons' on Christmas Eve: and almost precisely the same set of people to be assembled, too. With the exception of Mrs. Elton, of course. Even Mr. John Knightley, I believe, will be present; he is bringing Henry and John down from Brunswick Square to stay with their grandfather and aunt.

As some consolation for what may be going on in Harriet's funny little head I have ordered a good dinner on that night for the parlour boarders and myself. We will have treacle pudding, Harriet's favourite, and I have been promised a fine carp, which I intend to have stuffed. Perhaps we may play conundrums – no, that might not be very tactful; but I shall contrive something for their amusement.

And now here's yet another enigma. Alice, when she goes to the Post Office of a morning, tells me that instead of the good Bateses' Patty fetching their letters, (with whom she always enjoys a gossip) it is now Miss Fairfax, herself, who goes for the mail. Even in this damp weather. Yet she is supposed to be delicate and liable to catch cold. Since Alice tells me that Patty looks forward to her daily outing to the post office, there seems no reason why Miss Fairfax should usurp this duty.

So there is a puzzle for you and Mr. Pinkney. You with your mind for mysteries I suppose will say she is conducting a clandestine correspondence with an admirer. Perhaps he who sent the pianoforte? There! How is that for a conjecture? Am I not an apt pupil? Quite worthy of yourself, dear Charlotte.

Your affectionate sister,
M. Goddard

P.S. Miss Fairfax, by the way, is to stay on at her grandmother's for another two months. The Campbells are extending their visit to Ireland, and although they have–according to Miss Bates–pressed her to join them and offered to send servants, etc., she has chosen to remain in Highbury.

LETTER 38

From Mrs. Pinkney to Mrs. Goddard

Sloane Street
11 April 1814

Ha! my dear Mary, I am ahead of you. I knew already that the two little Knightley boys were going to their grandfather's. Mr. Wingfield, now he is aware of my connexion with Highbury, mentioned it as a subject of interest. He wondered if I knew how it had come about that Mrs. John Knightley was so over-concerned with matters of health; familiar as he is with her idiosyncracies, even he was astonished at a long list of instructions she showed him that she had written out for her sister. She evidently consulted him on several points of concern in comprising it. I told Mr. Wingfield that, even though I had never met him, I fancied Mr. Woodhouse was the cause. All I can say is, if Mrs. J. K. does not succeed in turning her children into valetudinarians, it will not be for want of trying.

Yes, you are indeed an apt pupil, my dear Mary. So Miss Fairfax is fetching the letters, is she? Undoubtedly it is a lover. Obviously a very rich one, if he can afford a Broadwood pianoforte; for presumably it must be the same person to whom she is writing. Could *that* be why she did not go to Ireland with the Campbells? Difficult to conceal a clandestine correspondence if one is a guest in somebody else's house.

Later: I had got no further than that, when I was interrupted by Charlotte, in great distress, coming hastily into the room to see me. As Mr. P. afterwards so truly observed, why is it that when everything is going along smoothly, and all appears to be plain

119

sailing, a storm will blow up and one's frail craft be beset by difficulties?

Such is the case with Charlotte. The odious great aunt, Lady Matthews, has written to Madame Dubois and declared that now Charlotte is about to be eighteen she will no longer pay her fees. She has asked Madame to find her a situation as governess, and proposes to wash her hands of her great niece entirely.

Although this development was not unexpected, it does not make it any less disagreeable. Much as Charlotte dislikes the school, at least it is a known evil. She dreads being sent out to an uncongenial family in some remote part of the kingdom; for one thing, the mails may be quite uncertain. At her tender age, and without references or experience, she is likely only to be employed where the people are not able to pay someone better qualified.

One would think that Madame might offer to keep her on to teach the little ones – but now that wretched woman is no longer to be *paid* for maintaining Charlotte, she wants her to be gone, and the sooner the better.

Looming over these concerns, however, and causing everything else to pale into insignificance as far as Charlotte is concerned, is the far more important question of Lieutenant Marlowe. She has not heard from him for three weeks; this is the longest period she has been without a letter. Whether this means he has thought better of the attachment, (which I privately think possible) or whether he is at sea and unable to communicate, which is what she hopes and believes, there is no means of discovering. Ever faithful and undaunted, she has continued to write to him, and he has now been apprised of this latest turn of events; though I do not know what he can or will do when he hears of it. Certainly, the Navy seems to have some very odd tasks at hand these days. Having wiped the French from the seas, I suppose there is not too much of a fighting nature left to be done except against the Americans. At the moment, as I pointed out to Charlotte, conditions are so uncertain, that until they and that villain Napoleon are finally vanquished, it is not a time for a young sailor even to *think* about marriage.

All this and more I discussed with her, offering as much sympathy and affection as was in my power, and keeping my more untoward thoughts to myself. After she had gone, and forlorn she looked I can tell you – Mr. Pinkney and I sat down to discuss the matter seriously.

You can imagine the dilemma this development has placed us in. She is too young and inexperienced (in our opinion) to be sent off alone to live and work among strangers. There seems to be no choice but to offer her a home here with us. Certainly we enjoy her visits in the afternoons, are both extremely fond of her, and of course are grateful to her for (unwittingly) bringing us together. But, ironically enough, *that* is the very reason we do not wish to have her in the house. We feel we have but just begun our honeymoon. Mr. Pinkney is particularly reluctant to have a third person continuously present to encroach upon our *tête-à-tête*.

We have been debating and deliberating over the business all morning – but the conclusion of our discourse is that in all decency, we cannot do less than invite her to live here.

In fact, dear Mary, I am finding myself in the position for which I once pitied you – the prospect of having to share my table and my parlour with an unmarried girl, for who knows how long a period.

We agreed that this was an offer better written than spoken directly. Accordingly I have composed a letter – as coming from both Mr. Pinkney and myself – asking her to come to us for as long as it suits her.

I made it as genuinely welcoming as possible, but did not send it off at once, deciding that I would write to you first, and that perhaps in putting down my thoughts on paper, I might gain a better perspective and understanding of my own very mixed feelings.

I find that nothing has changed. In common humanity here is something that must be done. I have just rung for Betty and shall ask her to take the letter over to the school.

I am tired and will not write more.

Yrs. ever,

C. Pinkney

LETTER 39

From Mrs. Goddard to Mrs. Pinkney

Highbury,
13 April 1814

I am sorry for your concern over Charlotte. Although you cannot expect me, who has been having large numbers of girls living here for the past seventeen years, to sympathize too much with your reluctance to have her in the house; especially considering on what good terms you have been and how often you have reiterated that you enjoyed her company. Still I *do* very much understand your wish to give all your attention to Mr. Pinkney, and his to be alone with you, with *that* I do sympathize.

I suggest that with a little contrivance and in the interests of domestic harmony, you establish one or two precedents: for example, that she remains a certain time in her own room every day, so that you may have some privacy: that occupations are found for her – could she help a little in the kitchen? It is important that she should feel useful. Of course she must have exercise, and she cannot go out alone in London, so you will be obliged to take her on your walks, unless you can spare Betty to go with her. I daresay in due time you will arrive at a system which suits you all, and I am sure it cannot last forever. I have more faith in Lieutenant Marlowe than you do. I do not for one moment believe that Charlotte will be an old maid.

It is, alas, very true that one has only to congratulate oneself on the smooth running of one's affairs, and it is as if Fate were listening, and determined to teach one a lesson for one's complaisance. Strange as it may seem, I, too, find myself in a domestic predicament which is causing me much distress.

It concerns my faithful servant, Alice, whom I daresay I have mentioned a great deal more often than you care to hear about her. But she is quite invaluable to me in many ways. Lately, though, we have had words on a number of occasions, for which I could not account.

The reason, however, has been becoming ever more obvious, and now the fact is plain to see. I took her aside into the parlour to ask what she proposed doing. Poor Alice broke down and wept in frustration and rage. The villain of the piece is an osler at the Crown, a handsome jackanapes with a bad reputation who has, over the years, got more than one girl into trouble. Alice is not young and how or why she succumbed to his blandishments is impossible to understand. Possibly he promised marriage, who knows? Of course now he denies all responsibility, and what can Alice do? If I had only my own feelings to consider, I would keep her here. But the parents of my young ladies would very much dislike having their innocent daughters exposed to this most flagrant breach of decorum.

I had thought she might return to her family, who live on a farm in the next parish. But she is afraid to ask them, her father being an irascible old man who has lately taken up Methodism. I have agreed to write the necessary letter on her behalf: explaining that I will be very ready to have her back after her confinement, provided she can in some way arrange for the child. When it is older, of whatever sex, I am sure it could be useful around the school, another generation of children will have come and gone, and she can adopt the brevet rank of "Mrs."

You speak of Napoleon. I fear not much heed is paid in Highbury to the great affairs of the world, save as they impinge on our own lives, and in your case, perhaps, on Charlotte's.

What else can I tell you?

The little Knightley boys have arrived. Miss Woodhouse is quite a devoted aunt to her sister's children. Harriet tells me that she has made them cardboard letters so that they can learn their spelling and play word games.

Then the handsome and captivating Frank Churchill is likely to be among us again soon. Mrs. Churchill has decided that Yorkshire is too cold for her. They are to remove to London for the summer, where it is hoped her health will improve with the change. Mr. Weston is full of happy anticipation at the prospect of seeing his son. Only sixteen miles! Nothing for a young man! He can ride down almost every day!

And speaking of the Westons, I do not believe I have mentioned the happy news which reached me privately (and in great secrecy through Harriet and Miss Woodhouse) that Mrs. Weston is to have a child. I cannot help but remark – thinking of my poor Alice, who is about the same age as Mrs. Weston – with what different expectations these two children are anticipated; one with pride and rejoicing – the other with shame and lamentation.

Yours aff.,

M. G.

LETTER 40

From Mrs. Pinkney to Mrs. Goddard

Sloane Street
15 April 1814

Happy Mrs. Weston! I remember your hoping that such an event would occur. Good fortune does seem to attend that woman. Well, if she is safely delivered, she will have everything her heart could desire. From what you say, she deserves it.

And in contrast – poor Alice. Poor woman! I suppose she could not resist this fellow. For her, a last chance; for him, another seduction; nothing more than a game in which she was bound to be the loser; for in spite of the proverb, what's sauce for the goose never was sauce for the gander.

You will be interested to hear about Charlotte. That same sturdy independence that constrained her to sit uncomplainingly on the outside of the coach, will not allow her to accept our offer.

She wrote me a very touching and grateful letter. She would always remember our kindness and how much she owed to us,

124

etc., etc. but, as she is eventually to be a governess, there is no point in putting off what is inevitable. Madame Dubois has listed her name at an agency, and she is expecting to hear of a situation before long.

I confess to very mixed emotions: pity, relief, guilt; concern and admiration for a brave soul.

I am persuaded that she cannot bear to face me, in case her resolve should break down, for she has not been near the house since. This does not make me feel any better, I assure you. I have been wondering if I ought not to write again, to press her. But Mr. P. is reluctant. "My dear," he says, "we have done our duty. Let us leave matters where they stand." Besides, he is actively looking, or his man of business is looking, for another house for us to occupy; so we hope to be removing from here before too long.

I must comfort myself with the thought that perhaps Charlotte will get into some good, kind family that appreciates her and makes her one of them, even as Miss Taylor, years ago, was taken in by the Woodhouses.

Mr. P. and I are beginning to go out in society in a modest way. One of his old Cambridge friends took us to a reception where I met many agreeable people. Though I suppose you will be amused when I tell you that society is no longer so absolutely necessary to me as it once was. In fact, we are finding ourselves very happy at home. Suddenly we have so much to talk about–a lifetime of talk to catch up on. Mr. Pinkney has begun to call me "Charlotte" in the modern way. Mr. Wingfield told me that Mr. John Knightley calls his wife, Isabella. I have not quite brought myself to address Mr. Pinkney by his Christian name, though I expect I shall in time.

He has been so kind–it was entirely his own idea–as to write to Admiral Seymour and inquire as to the whereabouts of Lieutenant Marlowe, and inform him of the young people's attachment. Since they were much in company together at Bath, it might interest him.

I hope you are successful in finding a new maid.

     Adieu,
      Charlotte

LETTER 41

From Mrs. Goddard to Mrs. Pinkney

Highbury,
17 April 1814

My dear Charlotte,

One does admire young Charlotte's fortitude in refusing your offer. It cannot have been easy. She must be a most admirable young woman. Let us hope an eligible situation presents itself soon.

Alice has now gone. Her father utterly refused to have her darken his door. So much for Christian charity! Fortunately I have been able to prevail upon a former servant, who worked here with Alice, and who is now married, to take her in. In a household of so many children, another will make not much difference, and the extra money will be very acceptable. I shall have to withdraw it from my little parlour-boarder nest-egg; but I cannot begrudge doing this much for one who has served me well and faithfully for so many years, and, who, when this trying affair is over, will do so again in her former reliable style, I feel sure.

Meanwhile, I am making inquiries about Highbury for a responsible servant, and Mrs. Martin, with whom I have reestablished some sort of communication, is kindly looking out for me among the farm girls in her parish. I am sorry to be tedious, burdening you with the details of this sad little story which is much on my mind at present.

I have seen the little Knightley boys out walking with their aunt: fine-looking children who have grown since Christmas, and who show no signs of ill-health! I suppose Henry, the elder, will eventually inherit Donwell Abbey, since his uncle, Mr. Knightley, seems to have no intention of marrying, and he must now be in his mid-thirties, at least.

Yours aff:ly,
M. G.

LETTER 42

From Mrs. Pinkney to Mrs. Goddard

Sloane Street
20 April 1814

My dear Mary,

You are concerned for your Alice, and I, equally so for Charlotte. After a lapse of three or four days, following my letter, she began coming over here again.

Negotiations are under way and it appears that a situation may have been found for her. It is as bad or worse than she feared; the family of an impoverished parson on a bleak moor in the north. There are three little girls for her to teach, but I imagine she will be not much more than a nursemaid.

Charlotte is stoic and resigned. She lives in hopes of a letter from Richard Marlowe, but none ever comes. She has given me her direction, and if and when a letter does arrive, I shall forward it to her, but who knows when that may be. The people to whom she is to go want her next week. I tell her not to despair, anything may happen in a week, and for her sake I most fervently hope it does. She is quite steadfast in her refusal of our offer and in her determination to support herself and be beholden to no one.

Mr. P.'s and my admiration for her is unbounded. He says the very best blood of the Royal Navy surely courses through her veins.

Adieu,
Charlotte

LETTER 43

From Mrs. Goddard to Mrs. Pinkney

25 April 1814

A hasty note dashed off on Mrs. Ford's counter. I was standing here buying some wool when a brilliant idea darted into my head.

At the same instant I spied through the window Mr. Frank Churchill, and hurried outside to enlist his co-operation. I had heard earlier that he was spending the day in Highbury, having ridden down from London for a few hours to see his friends here. It being essential that you receive this at once, I have borrowed pen and paper from Mrs. Ford, and am dashing it off for him to deliver to you personally this evening. He accepted the commission most graciously, assuring me that Sloane Street is not at all out of his way – that may be a polite fiction, I don't know. The Churchills are staying in Manchester Street.

But to get to the point; my brilliant thought is this: why not send Charlotte to me? She can help at the school in Alice's place.

I do pray that Frank Churchill will arrive with this in time to prevent her going to that unprosperous-sounding situation you mentioned.

I must stop. He is actually mounting his horse outside the window (just saying goodbye to Miss Bates and Miss Fairfax) and signalling to me that he is ready.

I will write a proper explanation this evening.

Yours,

M. G.

LETTER 43, continued

From Mrs. Goddard to Mrs. Pinkney

25 April 1814

My dear Charlotte,

Here is the explanation I promised you; but it will be brief, because I should go and supervise John and the maids. They have been cleaning the best carpet outside with tea leaves, and it is time it was brought indoors and turned end to end on the floor, and I *must* catch this evening's post.

Alice's province has included looking after the little ones – brushing their hair, overseeing their baths, hearing their prayers and their spelling. She has always had a room to herself, being senior and superior to the other servants. Her more menial tasks can easily be managed by a woman coming in daily.

In considering the situation of Alice I was set in the notion that she was a *servant* and with another such I would have to replace her. It was your mentioning that you felt young Charlotte's new position would be chiefly as 'nursemaid' which made me see her duties in a different light.

Let me know as soon as you can.

Yrs.,

M. Goddard

LETTER 44

From Mrs. Pinkney to Mrs. Goddard

Sloane Street
28 April 1814

Let you know *what* as soon as I can? I did not answer immediately. How could I?

Really, my dear Mary, a completely incomprehensible letter from you, giving me a list of Alice's former duties! Telling me how you clean your carpet! I honestly cannot say that such information is at the very forefront of my interest.

Nor do I care that Alice had a bedroom to herself. The domestic management of a school bears little resemblance, I am certain, to that of a private house. The work a servant is likely to have to do in a crowd of girls must be very different from the requirements of a mere couple. Betty is in a regular routine which suits her and is entirely satisfactory both to Mr. Pinkney and myself; besides, we have no little girls with hair to be brushed, or prayers to be heard. Dear Mary, I fear you have been overworking, and the worry of Alice has been too much for you.

Charlotte came in last night to say goodbye, since she was leaving early this morning on the coach for the north. She was very brave, but it was almost too much for *me*: to think she is gone, and that in all probability I shall not see her again. She has promised to write, and I to send on anything that may come from Lieutenant Marlowe.

She was quite determined on what she had decided, and I am trying to tell myself that it is all for the best, because, really, it would not do to have her permanently here with us.

Yours,

Charlotte

LETTER 45

From Mrs. Goddard to Mrs. Pinkney

Highbury,
30 April 1814

Dear Charlotte,

What do you mean, an incomprehensible letter?
Surely, although written in haste, the intention was perfectly plain. I do believe I was at least entitled to the civility of a reply. I hope it is not because you do not think my school is *elegant* enough for your *protégée* – niece of Lady Matthews – that you have not answered. I should have thought it would be vastly preferable to an unknown impoverished parsonage in the north. Although I could not have offered her a large salary, I daresay it was as good as she had conditioned for: and good food, comfort and kindness she *would* have been assured of. Besides, Highbury being only sixteen miles from London, would have been a very material advantage whenever Lieutenant Marlowe does appear: which I am convinced he will.

Well, you say she is gone, so there is nothing more to be done. I had told Mrs. Martin to cease keeping her eye out for me, feeling pretty well assured (how mistaken I was) of your young lady accepting the place with alacrity.

Yrs.,

M. G.

LETTER 46

From Mrs. Pinkney to Mrs. Goddard

Sloane Street
1 May 1814

My dearest Mary,

Something has obviously gone very wrong. I never received any letter from you offering a place to Charlotte in your school. I cannot understand what can have happened at the post office: usually so punctual and reliable. Mr. Pinkney is going to make enquiries.

Indeed, it has often crossed my mind how eligible such a situation would be for her, but since you did not offer, I did not feel I could presume to ask, especially knowing your same three teachers had been with you for many years; and, like you, it never occurred to me that she could take the place of a *servant*.

You might well think all is lost. But it is not.

Charlotte did leave for the *Northern Flyer* on the appointed morning. But when she got to the yard, and saw that once again she must sit outside on top, and for such an infinitely longer journey, too, her heart failed her; she felt sick and dizzy, was overcome by panic, and to her great mortification could not bring herself to mount the ladder. Not daring to go back to the school, knowing the sort of reception she would receive, she left her trunk at the Golden Cross, and somehow or other made her way to our house.

I heard the doorbell, and was astonished when Betty announced "Miss Gordon." Poor dear! She was so ashamed of her weakness and so afraid of troubling us as she explained the circumstance. She asked timidly if she might stay here until a place inside was available in three days time. Mr. P., who was present, asked if she had enough money, and with obvious reluctance she admitted she would be very grateful for a loan, since her way was paid on the outside only.

We sent Charles for her trunk, and then, as we were sitting here despondently this morning, your letter arrived. What a happy solution! Charlotte's joy knows no bounds; being at your school will satisfy her notions of pride and independence. Now I can think of her with you: happy and occupied – a great deal happier than she ever was with Madame Dubois. The very idea that I would consider that dreadful seminary superior to your school! Really, dear Mary! What can you be thinking of?

I shall write to the agency and cancel her engagement, couching the letter in formal terms, *Miss Gordon regrets she has accepted another situation.* I do not know if this information will get back to Madame Dubois. Quite likely, it will. I have advised Charlotte that we should be careful when she goes out of the house, so that she is not recognized by anyone from the school. It is a case of avoiding trouble. Once she is safely settled in Highbury, I suppose the great aunt should be notified, though I do not know why one should trouble oneself since she never troubles herself over Charlotte.

Let us know when you would like her. She is eager to begin. To celebrate, Mr. P. is taking us tonight, Charlotte included, to *The Merchant of Venice* at the Drury Lane Theatre. It will be the first time Mr. P. and I have been to a play together, and I am in great anticipation of a pleasant evening.

I am so happy for Charlotte, for myself (now my scruples of conscience are quite overcome) and for *you*, because you are not out of your head, as I supposed.

Adieu,

Charlotte

P.S. A thought has occurred. Someone must accompany Charlotte down to Highbury – *and why not me?* I shall wait for a suitable moment to broach the subject.

LETTER 47

From Mrs. Goddard to Mrs. Pinkney

Highbury,
3 May 1814

I owe you a profound apology, my dear Charlotte. It was not the Post Office, but that reprehensible Frank Churchill who is at fault. What a specious young man! So charming as he was, so smiling and so ready and willing to do me a favour. He was here, in Highbury, you see, and I gave him the letter, because it was vital that it reached you at once. Well, I never did think much of his *character*, remembering his reluctance to visit Mrs. Weston, and his going up to London for a haircut. Now I think a good deal less. I suppose one day his valet will discover the scrap of paper in his pocket and throw it away as of no importance, little knowing that perhaps a young lady's ultimate happiness depended upon it.

Well, I will not dwell on the matter further. How fortunate that Charlotte could not face the top of the coach. No wonder, after her last experience! Pray send (or bring) her as soon as you like. Highbury may not be an ideal or even a permanent solution, but it will give her some respite before she is overtaken by events, whatsoever they may be: her father re-appearing . . . Lieutenant Marlowe proposing . . . whatever improbable fantasy a young lady is likely to be dreaming of in her fertile imagination.

I cannot believe I may actually see *you*, yourself, my dearest Charlotte. The prospect is too delightful for words. But we have been disappointed so many times, I shall not allow myself to count on it until you are actually here.

What other news do I have? Oh, yes, the Churchills have moved from London, where, as you know, they had settled – supposedly for the spring – to Richmond. They have discovered a well-recommended apothecary there and taken a furnished house for the months of May and June. London and its noise did not suit Mrs. Churchill's nerves. I imagine that nothing suits Mrs. Churchill for long. Does this trivial piece of information interest you? It should, because the consequence is that Frank Churchill (*not* in my good books at the moment) will be that much nearer to Highbury. Since the Churchills have been in London, he has succeeded in getting down here only once – on that memorable occasion. Now, the young people are all talking about the proposed ball as a certainty.

So glad all is happily resolved, my dear Charlotte,

Ever yours most affectionately,
Mary

LETTER 48

From Mrs. Pinkney to Mrs. Goddard

Sloane Street
7 May 1814

Good news, my dear Mary.

Mr. P., has suggested *himself*, without a word from me, that I should accompany Charlotte to Highbury. He asks, however, that I stay away only three nights. He cannot spare me for longer. I teased him a bit, asked him why he had always refused my request to go there before.

"Because, my dear, I was afraid you might not come back again."

"And what makes you think I will come back now, sir?"

He looked very solemn, then I caught his eye and we both burst out laughing. We perfectly understand each other.

Oh, my dear Mary, how foolish and selfish I was: how miserable then – and how happy now.

We had a splendid evening at the theatre – Edmund Kean played Shylock. Such acting I never hope to see surpassed. But my thoughts now are of Highbury – not of London.

Just think that after so many years you and I are to meet at last! Will we find each other very much changed? Are you thinner or fatter than I remember? Is your hair grey from the care of your young ladies, and the vicissitudes of life in Highbury, where nothing ever happens?

Yes, it does. You are to have a ball. I am very glad, and expect a full account afterwards. Will you dance with Mr. Frank Churchill? Or cut him dead with a twitch of your shoulders?

I will not bring Charlotte down for a few days yet. She has caught a bad cold, and you would not want that spread among your girls. Then Betty told me privately that her underclothes are in a shocking state. I would like to equip her properly before she goes to you, and this will take me a few days. Then, oh joy, I shall see you!

This slight delay happens to be rather convenient, since old friends Mr. Grenville and I used to know in Yorkshire are coming to town; Mr. P. and I have promised to dine with them. If it is anything like our last outing, it will be very enjoyable. Two days ago we had a most succulent supper. It was Ladies' Night at Mr. Pinkney's whist club. He said how proud he was to introduce me as his wife, and how he relished the expression on their faces when they met me. I refrained from remarking that no doubt they wondered why this introduction had never taken place before. Things have changed, indeed! How vividly I remember our mutual embarrassment when the Admiral was quizzing me about our marriage. Be that as it may, Mr. P. enjoyed himself so much he threw caution to the winds. There was roast goose and good wine and pigeon pies, and he ate and drank like he used to do in the old days. I have said to him that this morning we must go for a very long walk as penance for our intemperance.

Yours very affectionately,
Charlotte

P.S. Everyone in town is talking about Napoleon being exiled to Elba. Who would have deemed it possible a year ago? Of course we still have those unruly Americans to contend with.

LETTER 49

From Mrs. Goddard to Mrs. Pinkney

Highbury,
12 May 1814

So you are actually coming! My *dearest* Charlotte! Most good of Mr. Pinkney to spare you. Please extend to him my thanks and gratitude. As to my appearance, I seldom look in a looking-glass and I absolutely decline to describe myself. You will have to wait and see, when you come, what I look like.

Prepare for a letter of joy and pleasure, for it is to be entirely about the ball.

I did receive an invitation. Mr. Woodhouse is to have Mrs. Bates to keep him company. Dear old man, fond as I am of him, I am glad to be spared on this occasion. So here I sit, dressed in my best black satin, and wearing my mother's gold locket (you remember the one? set with my father's hair) waiting in the parlour with Miss Bickerton for the moment of setting out for the Crown. What a treat this is going to be for us all.

Harriet has already left, having been called for by Miss Woodhouse in the carriage. She very much wanted to ask if Miss Bickerton and I could accompany them. I was obliged to be quite firm. "Thank you, dear child," said I, "but it would be absolutely improper. You were invited quite half an hour earlier than we were. I expect Mrs. Weston wishes Miss Woodhouse to be there first, before the regular crowd of guests; she is, after all, like a daughter to her."

So they departed, and we remained, and now it is time for us to go also. Such delightful anticipation! I shall continue.

Later: Dear me, it is now half past two in the morning, and I cannot begin to sleep, so I have lit my candle and am writing to you. I am not used to so much excitement. Besides, I am disturbed by a rather untoward incident which quite spoiled the ball for me.

Miss Bickerton and I easily made our way to the Crown, it was spotting a little with rain, but not enough to signify, and, being May, it was not yet quite dark. We arrived to find a number of people standing in a circle round a pleasant fire, for the evening was cool. After paying our respects to our host and hostess, we joined this circle. Mr. Frank Churchill was in another part of the room, talking to Miss Woodhouse. He seemed distracted, did not notice me arriving, and even if he did, I am persuaded he has entirely forgotten the incident of the undelivered letter. Mr. and Mrs. Elton walked in shortly afterwards, she looking extremely fashionable in lace and pearls. There was a little bustle on their arrival. It appeared they were to have brought Miss Bates and Miss Fairfax: Mr. Weston and his son were most concerned. The deficiency was soon remedied, however, the carriage was sent for them. I heard Mrs. Elton declaiming that their horses were "so extremely expeditious," and that "we drive faster than anybody." Just the sort of boastful remark Mrs. Elton *would* make: so full of self-importance as she is. Dear Charlotte, you will think me spiteful to be telling you this, but I cannot forgive either her, or her husband, their treatment of Harriet – of which, more anon. From her behaviour you would have thought that *she* was the hostess of the ball, and it was *her* province to greet the guests; anybody less kind and forbearing than Mrs. Weston would have very much resented it.

Very soon afterwards Miss Bates and Miss Fairfax arrived, Miss Fairfax with beautifully arranged hair – I understand she does it herself. Miss Bates was quite full of the joy of being at a ball, and the transformation Mrs. Weston had wrought in the dingy premises of the Crown. I must admit, however, that her mother's spectacles and her mother's shawl did not escape a mention in her speech of greeting to Mrs. Weston. When you come next week, dear Charlotte, you must certainly meet Miss

138

Bates. But you must promise me to keep your countenance. Under no circumstances would one wish to hurt her feelings.

Soon afterwards the set was forming and the music beginning. Miss Bickerton's hand was claimed by the son of my writing master, and I, not wishing to sit with the old people in the cardroom, remained by the fire with Dr. and Mrs. Hughes. We drank wine and watched the dancing. Mr. Knightley stood near us. Such a fine upstanding man. I wondered that he did not himself dance. Of course he is older than the likes of Frank Churchill and Mr. Elton. Still, that should not prevent his dancing, but I don't think he cares for it. I suspect he would rather have been at Donwell Abbey discussing the crops with William Larkins. All the young people had partners. The numbers seemed to have been excellently contrived by Mrs. Weston. Mr. Knightley, had he danced, would have made an extra man. And so the evening went along in fine style, until the last two dances before supper; then something happened, dear Charlotte, which, calm and composed as I normally am, really made my blood boil.

My little Harriet was sitting out – the only young lady without a partner. I wondered how this was possible? Then I saw that Mr. Elton, who had hitherto danced every dance, was strolling about amongst the bystanders, frequently passing near Harriet, looking straight at her, or through her, I should rather say, and never asking her to join the set. Mrs. Weston approached him,

"Do not you dance, Mr. Elton?"

"Most readily, Mrs. Weston, if you will dance with me."

I could not hear exactly what was said next, but she was plainly suggesting he stand up with Harriet. He shook his head, I saw him shoot a gleeful glance at his wife as he stalked off towards the cardroom.

Poor little Harriet looked mortified beyond bearing and Mrs. Weston most distressed. How dare he! He, who only five months ago was contributing *Courtship* to Harriet's book. I was on the point of rising and going over to her when Mr. Knightley, of all people, moved decisively forward and led her into the set; and the next thing I knew she was flying about looking as if she were in a state of perfect bliss.

What if she had been in love with Mr. Elton? So was every other young woman in the town. Did she deserve this snub? Why should my harmless little girl be thus publicly humiliated?

After supper, to everybody's surprise, Mr. Knightley and Miss Woodhouse stood up together. They made such a very handsome, elegant, couple, and they danced so gracefully that everybody was much struck. I imagine it is because we are all inclined to think of them as brother and sister – there being that close connexion between the families, and Mr. Knightley spends so much time at Hartfield. Certainly all eyes were upon them. I believe there must be about sixteen years difference in their ages. When I first arrived in Highbury, he was a young man, and she but a small child.

Before supper Miss Bates had stolen away unnoticed to put her mother to bed, and come back again afterwards. One does laugh at her. But she is such a good soul – a carriage to arrive, but none to convey her home to her duties. She said that she had stout shoes, however, and did not get wet feet. I was seated near them at supper and I heard her tell Miss Fairfax how her mother's evening had gone. James had brought her safely home from Hartfield all right, but there had been a severe disappointment. Mrs. Bates had not been so lucky as we had been at the time of the Coles' dinner party. Mr. Woodhouse had not allowed her to eat the beautiful dish of sweetbreads and asparagus that Serle had prepared. Most disappointing. He thought it undercooked. *Our* supper at the Crown was excellent, especially the soup.

Apart from the Eltons, then, it was a very good ball.

To think I shall see you very soon!

Your affectionate sister,
M. Goddard

LETTER 50

From Mrs. Pinkney to Mrs. Goddard

Sloane Street
15 May 1814

My dear Mary,

Oh, the vile creature! Everything you tell me about that man and his wife confirms the impression they made on me at Bath. Obviously he set out deliberately to humiliate Harriet. But why would a man wish to humiliate a young woman for being in love with him? You would think he might be endeared or flattered by the circumstance. No, Mr. P. thinks he wanted to injure more than Harriet? Someone close to her. It could not have been you, it must have been Miss Woodhouse. Mr. Elton was demonstrating how utterly beneath his notice her little friend, Harriet, was. I suppose it still rankles – Miss W.'s refusal of him – and *her* expectation that *Harriet* would be his choice. At least that is what we surmise, and what other explanation can there be? I suppose this incident quite spoiled your pleasure in the ball, and I am very sorry for it. I wish that man and his wife would go into their vicarage, shut the door behind them and stop tormenting you, and, I imagine, others by their actions.

We have been almost dissipated lately. The old friends from Yorkshire came as arranged. We had a grand dinner together of suckling pig and soles, and much laughter and conviviality as well. Mr. Pinkney had met them before. I fear we again both ate and drank more than we ought. Then there was the annual banquet of a learned society to which Mr. P. belongs. I hope this over-indulgence will have no ill effect. Mr. Wingfield has been quite displeased with us. I try not to divulge all the family secrets, but,

141

as I told you, he has a way of drawing one out and making one disclose that which one would rather not. Most disconcerting.

Charlotte is very amenable. Spends her evenings sewing her new undergarments with Betty. Her cold is almost gone, but I think I should wait until she has got rid of it entirely. We now plan to stay at home until I bring her down to Highbury. I am not quite comfortable about leaving her so much alone.

Expect us within the next few days.

Yrs. very aff:ly,
Charlotte

LETTER 51

From Mrs. Goddard to Mrs. Pinkney

Highbury,
17 May 1814

My dear Charlotte,

I am glad you are enjoying yourselves with the various entertainments that London offers, and I am delighted that it falls to your lot and not to mine. You have your compensations for living in London, but they would not compensate *me*. The song of birds I would always choose over the rumble of wheels on cobblestones, and the scent of new-mown hay I must ever prefer to the sickening smells of a town. Though I have to tell you that even here, even in our peaceful little Highbury, the devil will intrude on paradise and shocking things can happen.

It is now several days since it occurred, but it is still an ardent topic of conversation around the tea tables of Highbury, and at the actual time it was a *very* alarming incident. It would have been considered nothing, I'm sure, in London, where ruffians and thieves abound in the streets, but in this small place everyone has been talking with horror of what *might have been* if the girls had not been rescued in the nick of time.

The morning after the ball Harriet and Miss Bickerton set out for a walk. I was glad to see Harriet paying this attention to her fellow parlour boarder, who has been left very much on her own lately. They were in high spirits chattering away about the previous evening.

An hour later I was outside, overseeing the maids, for the sun was shining and it was the day of our great wash, when suddenly I descried the figure of a young woman running towards us along the road. As she came nearer, I saw that it was Miss Bickerton, panting, red of face, and in a state of hysterics.

"Good Heavens, what has happened?" I cried, hastening forward to meet her. "Where is Miss Smith?" It was some moments before she could recover herself sufficiently to reply. Meanwhile, you may imagine my anxiety and impatience.

"Oh, Mrs. Goddard," she sobbed, "a most terrible thing. A mob of gypsies, a whole pack of them, accosted us. Harriet gave them sixpence, but they wanted more and began to be very threatening. I was so frightened I jumped over the hedge and ran up the hill."

"What?" cried I. "You did not leave Miss Smith alone?"

"I could not help it. I felt sure she would follow me, I do not know why she did not."

"Good Heavens, then I must send after her at once," and I called to John, who was lifting the washtubs for the maids.

"No, no, she's all right," gasped Miss Bickerton, preventing me. "Mr. Frank Churchill is with her."

"Mr. Frank Churchill!"

"Mrs. Goddard, it was like a miracle. He just appeared out of the blue. From where I stood on the hill I could hear him speaking sharply to the gypsies and ordering them off. Away they ran, like scared cats. Serve them right, too."

Agitated as I was, I knew Harriet would be quite safe with him, and was too relieved to say more to Miss Bickerton. Poor foolish, insipid creature that she is, she must have been quite aware of my opinion of her conduct. Almost immediately Mr.

Woodhouse's James arrived with messages that Harriet was safe, and would stay the night at Hartfield if her things could be sent over. So ended our great alarum. But, as you may believe, the incident is still the subject of tea visits for all the good folk of Highbury.

I shall be pleased to have young Charlotte as soon as may be, more especially because her coming will bring *you*, dear sister.

Yrs. most aff:ly,

M. Goddard

LETTER 52

From Mrs. Pinkney to Mrs. Goddard

Sloane Street
24 May 1814

My dear Mary,

I have not written sooner because I was hoping not to have to write as I am doing. I am afraid there is a change of plans. Charles will bring Charlotte down on the coach tomorrow. She should arrive soon after you receive this letter.

Alas, I am very sorry, but I cannot possibly leave poor Mr. Pinkney. All that good-living has had the consequence we feared. He has been laid low with the most severe attack of gout he has ever experienced. Mr. Wingfield calls frequently, and I have been with the poor patient every moment trying to divert his mind and alleviate the pain. Of course it does not make it any easier to bear that he brought it on himself, and I believe when he gets the better of this he will never – so he swears, over-indulge again.

Your account of the gypsies in *itself*, as you suggest, we could not take too seriously compared to the atrocities committed every day in the streets of London. We can well imagine, however, the stir it must have created in Highbury circles where the theft of a chicken from a poultry yard no doubt looms large as a heinous crime.

But as far as the *social* aspect was concerned, we were most amused by the romantic possibilities of the fair young lady being saved by the handsome young man. As Mr. P. pointed out, is it not curious that your little Harriet should be "rescued" on two successive days by two different gentlemen? On the one hand from the hateful Mr. Elton, and on the other from the dangerous gypsies.

Which was the more formidable adversary in the mind of your flighty little girl, it would be diverting to discover. We would not put it past her to fall in love with either of them on this account – rather as our Charlotte did when saved from falling by Lieutenant Marlowe. (Still silence from that quarter, by the way). We also wonder which of these two gentleman will be the one to be chosen? Because quite inevitably, having failed to win Mr. Elton and having rejected Robert Martin, she is need of *someone* to love. A girl like Harriet cannot be without. Well, Mary, which do you wager? Mr. Knightley or Frank Churchill?

Mr. Pinkney is very miserable and most pathetically grateful that I have elected to stay with him. Nobly, he did offer to part with me, but I would not hear of it on any account. He needs all the comfort I can give him.

Your affectionate sister,
Charlotte

P.S. I had not sealed this when Mr. P. made a suggestion. He proposes we *both* come down to Highbury in August! Your pupils will be on holiday and you will have leisure to give to us. He fully intends that his attack will be over by then. He is rigidly adhering to Mr. Wingfield's prescriptions with absolute determination to recover. He is quite as eager to see you as I am. It will be an excellent chance for us to exchange the heats (and stinks and noise) of London for the scents and birdsong of the Garden of England in Surry.

LETTER 53

From Mrs. Goddard to Mrs. Pinkney

Highbury,
30 May 1814

My dear Charlotte,

I did not answer yours at once, thinking you would like to know how young Charlotte had settled in; and I knew you would have heard from your Charles that she had arrived safely.

Of course I was disappointed that you could not bring her yourself, but I am very glad that you are staying with Mr. Pinkney. You know my views on this subject. I trust he will soon get the better of this indisposition, and then I shall, indeed, look forward to welcoming you *both* in August.

That will be an ideal time of year as far as I am concerned. The three teachers will be away – they are taking lodgings at Brighton. We can have a long visit, and I shall be able to enjoy your company undisturbed from having to attend to some crisis or other in the school.

I recognized Charlotte at once from your description, only I think she is much prettier than you had led me to believe. Her hair is very red, but I would call it more copper than carrot, and it curls so delightfully and is so abundant, I would say it was quite her chief beauty.

She seems a very nicely-spoken, unaffected young woman, understandably a little nervous coming into this, her first situation, and evidently wanting very much to please. She talked warmly of your and Mr. Pinkney's kindness and said your encouragement and friendship had given her a confidence in herself she entirely lacked before. I did my best to make her feel easy, and as it happened she had not been many minutes in the house before she had an opportunity of showing her abilities.

There had been tears and an upset which was still going on when Charlotte arrived, and which she could not help seeing and over-hearing even while I was greeting her. Poor little Sukey had lost her favourite doll, the last present from her mother, and her dearest possession. But Charlotte, even while her trunk was carrying upstairs, went to her, and taking her by the hand said, "Come, dry your tears, Sukey, I'll help you find Maggie. Tell me where you've been and where you last remember going." We had all searched in vain, I may say. But Charlotte found the doll under a lilac bush in a secluded nook in the garden. It had been taken there by two of the younger girls for a secret tea party. They were afraid to own up, but your sympathetic Charlotte, being used to a school and the ways and means of children, by kindly probing with great tact and sympathy, extracted the truth. Sukey has consequently become her everlasting, willing, slave.

Well, it was a good start for Charlotte; that she should have succeeded where others had failed. She is much taken with the school, everything in so different a style from the seminary of Madame Dubois evidently. She kept exclaiming, "Oh, Mrs. Goddard, how comfortable, how *nice* everything is!" which I found rather endearing, of course.

She was particularly struck that she is to have a bedroom to herself (Alice's) with curtains on the windows and a *mat* to step onto when she gets out of bed.

At dinner she remarked on the boiled mutton and steamed puddings and the ample quantity provided. The poor child seems to have led a life of complete privation under that woman. She is too thin, as you suggest, but I hope to fatten her up. I am extremely pleased with her, and will do all I can to see that she is happy here at Highbury.

Miss Nash has offered to take her under her wing. I had hoped Harriet might befriend her, but Harriet is so much occupied at Hartfield that she is very little here.

In fact, I confess to being quite in the dark as to what is going on. The other morning a strange little incident occurred.

147

Passing through the hall, I saw, thrown across a chair, a shawl and a small parcel. Now tidiness is a virtue I do try very hard to inculcate in my young ladies. No one likes to live in a disordered house. I was about to pick these things up and take them away, when Harriet came flying down the staircase and cried out that they were hers.

"Harriet," I said, "you know very well I do not like things left lying about."

"To be sure," she said, and she was very sorry, but she was on her way out to Hartfield, and had forgot her handkerchief, and had just gone upstairs for a moment to fetch one.

She then snatched up her things – but not before I saw that the parcel was labelled, *Most precious treasures*.

I am afraid it is more of her nonsense. But since she was going to Hartfield, perhaps Miss Woodhouse will talk some sense into her.

I was quite shocked when I read your suggestion that she might fall in love with either Mr. Knightley or Frank Churchill. Neither of them would look at her for one moment, I feel sure. Still your having put the idea into my head, I would not put it past the silly girl. After all, she did not think Mr. Elton beyond her reach. O, alas, for Robert Martin.

Ever yours aff:ly,

M. Goddard

LETTER 54

From Mrs. Pinkney to Mrs. Goddard

Sloane Street
London
6 June 1814

My dear Mary,

Pray forgive my long silence. I have been very busy with Mr. Pinkney and his gout, and have not had time or inclination for writing.

I felt certain that young Charlotte would please you, and can safely assure you that she will continue to do so. She is a girl who improves on acquaintance, and who will not forfeit the good impression she has already made.

She has written me a most enthusiastic letter. Your warm welcome and the happy atmosphere of your school being a delightful contrast to that of her late unregretted establishment. The only flaw in her enjoyment is the silence from Richard Marlowe. But I gather she has no doubts of his fidelity and is living for the moment when she shall hear from him. When she does, *if* she does, I will send it on to Highbury immediately.

I am glad to say Mr. Pinkney is better. Although not able to walk yet, he is not in so much pain. Casting about in my mind for something to amuse him while he sits with his leg up, I hit upon the idea of giving him to peruse all the letters that you have ever written to me since we were first married. We have often talked, in fact we constantly talk, about you and Highbury. I have read parts aloud to him, from time to time, but he has never, until now, seen the actual letters in which you describe, in detail, the particulars of the enigmas and mysteries pertaining to the good people there. You do not object, I hope, dear Mary? He is expecting to make some miraculous discovery in the course of his perusal.

You are well aware of the excellent understanding which now subsists between my husband and myself; how we laugh that we could ever have had such misconceptions of each other. Nevertheless, it may surprise you to learn that I included *all* your early letters, even those in which you admonish me to be a better wife. I was not afraid or ashamed of doing so, because the real regard in which we *now* hold each other is so well-established that I thought he would be entertained to read these reminders of a state of affairs that no longer exists. I am proud to claim that he *now* finds me a perfectly satisfactory wife in *every* respect, as I do him, a husband.

He is quite different from Mr. Grenville, more scholarly, less fond of large parties, but still he has been quite willing to effect some changes to oblige me. We have become very comfortable and pleasant together, and as I grow older I find constant company is no longer so *absolutely* necessary to my happiness. Yes, Mary, I admit it. I *have* changed, but then so has my husband.

I hope I have not bored you with what you already know, but you played a prominent part in our reconciliation with your good advice, for which we both of us thank you.

Adieu,

Charlotte

LETTER 55

From Mrs. Goddard to Mrs. Pinkney

Highbury,
12 June 1814

You must, indeed, be very sure of yourself, my dear Charlotte, to have given Mr. Pinkney all my letters to read. Luckily he

cannot see your early ones to me: full of complaints and grievances and talking about going mad!

I certainly never thought, when I wrote as I did, that he would
ever see all my little domestic concerns and gossips. I do not know
that I am entirely pleased that he should do so. What one writes
to a sister, one does not necessarily write to her (unknown)
husband; but if it gives you satisfaction I will say no more.

Well, I look forward to August. Meanwhile, life in Highbury
jogs along. Frank Churchill comes fairly often over from Richmond. Harriet said that the other evening, on their walk after
dinner, she and Miss Woodhouse and Mr. Knightley had met up
with Miss Bates and Miss Fairfax and the Westons. They joined
forces and were walking together, when they saw Mr. Perry on
horseback in the distance. Frank Churchill remarked that he
understood he would soon be setting up his carriage – something
I never heard of. When was this to be? inquired Frank Churchill.
Then, since everybody expressed surprise, and none of the others
had ever heard of such a proposal, he decided that he must have
dreamt it. Even Harriet thought this was very odd. Then Miss
Bates chimed in to say that, indeed, it was not supposed to be
known in *general*, it was rather a secret, in fact, but there *had* been
some talk at one time of such a possibility. Mrs. Perry had been
trying to prevail upon her husband. Everybody expressed interest.
Harriet said Frank's father thought it strange that he, not living in
Highbury, could have dreamed such a thing, a thing which was
actually under active consideration. My dear Charlotte, this is all
very trifling, it shows my want of news to fill up a letter; still it
does seem as if there is more here than meets the eye. After that
they went back to Hartfield for tea, and while they were sitting
round the table, Frank Churchill proposed a game with the letters
Miss Woodhouse had made for her nephews.

With the object of testing out *your* theory, Charlotte, that
Harriet is likely to be in love with one or other of her rescuers,
and since they were both present on this occasion, I asked, "And
who was quickest at the game? Mr. Frank Churchill or Mr.
Knightley?"

Harriet said Mr. Knightley had sat a little apart, and not really joined in, but Mr. Frank Churchill and Miss Woodhouse had been laughing very much together and that they, or *he*, had kept pushing letters at Miss Fairfax, who looked very provoked, and, catching her aunt's eye, they had got up and gone home. Harriet said she saw one word. It was *blunder*. She did not know why this word, and others Frank Churchill pushed in her direction should have angered Miss Fairfax. Another little quiz for you, dear Charlotte.

The young people are planning a strawberry picnic to Donwell Abbey, and also an exploring party to Box Hill. Such delights would never have come in Harriet's way before she met Miss Woodhouse.

Ever yours aff:ly,
M. Goddard

LETTER 56

From Mrs. Pinkney to Mrs. Goddard

Sloane Street
18 June 1814

My dear Mary,

Goodness, is even Mr. Perry, the apothecary, contemplating a carriage, while the Pinkneys remain without. Things have come to a pretty pass.

Well! I have a striking announcement to make: with his good chess brain and having pieced all the clues together, Mr. Pinkney has arrived at the following verdict:

GUILTY!
Miss Fairfax and Mr. Frank Churchill of
being secretly engaged to one another.

What say you to that, Mrs. Goddard? Are you not astonished at his brilliance? He concludes they cannot be openly engaged, as of course Mrs. Churchill would never consent to giving up her beloved young man to another woman; and Frank, unless under her roof, is penniless. Here is Mr. Pinkney's evidence, deduced entirely from your letters:

1. When Frank Churchill went to London to get his hair cut, and came back in such good spirits, "as if he had achieved something miraculous" were your words, he had ordered the pianoforte, which arrived two days later on St. Valentine's Day.

2. The remark he made that, "only true affection" could have prompted including the music, was a reference to himself – an indirect declaration of love. Why should Miss Fairfax blush otherwise?

3. Who else does Miss Fairfax know rich enough to buy her an instrument?

4. Then there is the enigma of the Post Office. Did Alice indicate whether Jane Fairfax still goes to fetch the letters when Frank Churchill is actually staying with the Westons in Highbury? But whether she does or does not, really might not signify. They still may wish to communicate privately, being, we assume, never alone together. When they are in public they must attempt to conceal their attachment by a display of indifference, while Frank Churchill makes a point of flirting with Miss Woodhouse. (This last must be very hard on Miss Fairfax, in my opinion, and also on Miss Woodhouse, if she should be at all attracted to him – I should hardly have thought the game was worth the candle.)

5. But Jane Fairfax must have felt it was. Remember how she chose to stay on at her grandmother's, instead of having what one would have thought the very great pleasure and novelty of visiting her very dear friends in Ireland? What was the superior attraction of Highbury? *Frank Churchill.*

6. And, speaking of games, even your most recent letter mentions something which Mr. Pinkney's sharp eyes alighted on. The word *blunder*, which so much annoyed Miss Fairfax that she persuaded her aunt they should go home. We presume that she must have written to Frank about Mr. Perry's carriage, and then he made the "blunder" of mentioning what nobody else was aware of.

7. Lastly, you notice that *he* did not appear in Highbury until *she* did. Remember his many delays, postponements and excuses? To pay his respects to his father's new wife was evidently not a sufficient motive. The inducement he was waiting for was *Jane Fairfax*.

Mr. Pinkney rests his case. Have I not a clever husband? He is quite delighted with himself and glad to have had something to occupy his mind.

Adieu,

Charlotte

LETTER 57

From Mrs. Goddard to Mrs. Pinkney

Highbury,
26 June 1814

No. Quite wrong, my dear Charlotte. Clever and amusing as it is, Mr. Pinkney's hypothesis simply will not do. I shall reply in the same style as your letter.

1. At the strawberry picnic, which took place at Donwell three days ago, Miss Fairfax left early, before Frank Churchill had even arrived. Would she not have waited to see him if there had been any attachment between them? My source of information is Harriet, who was of the party.

2. Again, the day before yesterday at the excursion to Box Hill, which I told you was in contemplation: according to Harriet, Miss Woodhouse and Frank Churchill "flirted together excessively." So excessively that many of the party were quite disgusted and walked off, including Jane Fairfax. Harriet also said, that with reference to Mr. and Mrs. Elton (and I suppose also to himself and Miss Fairfax) Frank Churchill made the remark that an acquaintance formed at a watering-place – as those two couples each had done – will be "all guess and luck – and will generally be ill-luck." You must admit that is hardly the kind of gallant remark a lover would make to his intended. Very wounding, I would say. He must have been in a very curious mood. Apparently he also declared he would go abroad for two years and when he returned Miss Woodhouse was to have found him a wife exactly "like herself." Make of this what you will, it hardly comprehends an engagement to Miss Fairfax.

3. Finally, the lady in question has accepted a situation as governess at a Mrs. Smallwood's, an acquaintance of Mrs. Elton's sister in the neighbourhood of Maple Grove. She leaves Highbury shortly.

I beg your pardon, Charlotte my dear, for pouring cold water, a positive douche – on Mr. Pinkney's "discovery" – but there are far too many flaws in his case; it is obvious there is no engagement there.

I confess the pianoforte is an unsolved mystery, and Mr. Pinkney's explanation of the expedition to get a haircut is certainly most inventive. But for lack of further evidence I think we will have to be satisfied that it was indeed a present from Colonel Campbell.

Speaking of the Box Hill excursion, Harriet told me something which quite shocked me. I do not know quite how to put it, or even if I should repeat what is really gossip.

But having whetted your appetite, and knowing the interest you take in the affairs of Highbury, I suppose I must proceed. I asked Harriet if she had enjoyed herself, if it had been a success ful expedition. She, to my surprise, said it had not. That everyone seemed out of sorts and at odds with one another. It appears that Miss Woodhouse was quite rude – almost insolent – to Miss Bates. They were playing conundrums or some sort of game in which everybody had to say something, and Miss Woodhouse made a witticism about there being a difficulty: Miss Bates not knowing when to stop. Miss Bates reddened, and was obviously hurt. True, it may be, but not at all what one would ever wish to *say*. Harriet said that later, as she and Miss Woodhouse were getting into the carriage, Mr. Knightley caught up with them and quite reprimanded Miss Woodhouse for uttering such a thing to an old friend who was poor, and who, at one time, when her father was Vicar, had been in very different circumstances and had been looked up to in Highbury. Miss Woodhouse did not reply, but as the carriage advanced down the hill, Harriet saw the tears streaming down her cheeks.

That Emma Woodhouse, the elegant, charming, superior Miss Woodhouse should be so affected by Mr. Knightley's disapprobation, and that he should presume to rebuke her, was an idea quite new to me. I suppose an elder brother – as he must think of himself as being – does feel he has that prerogative.

Young Charlotte continues well and seems happy. If anything, she is *too* anxious to please, and works too hard. But I cannot persuade her to do less. She asks every day if there is any post, poor child. Meanwhile, she declares she likes to keep busy. She even insisted on helping with the spring cleaning. We were taking the curtains outside and hanging them on the clothes line to brush; a lot of heavy work, climbing, carrying and lifting. But you are not interested in this. Certainly it is delightful to hear the laughter of the little ones at bedtime when she plays with them and tells them stories – something they have missed lately under the care of my poor sad Alice.

Ever yours aff:ly,
M. Goddard

P.S. My dear Charlotte, some astonishing news has just come. Mrs. Churchill is dead! An express arrived at Randalls this afternoon. Poor woman. We have all been completely mistaken, evidently. The imaginary complaints – as we were all pleased to think they were – must actually have been genuine. How one feels for Mr. Churchill and Frank Churchill. The sudden shock of it must affect them both excessively. Nothing is known at present of arrangements and possibilities.

LETTER 58

From Mrs. Pinkney to Mrs. Goddard

Sloane Street
London
28 June 1814

My dear Mary,

So Mrs. Churchill is dead. I will not attempt any empty protestations of regret. She has been an hateful woman all her life, and caused much suffering to others. As Mr. P. remarked, many an estimable person is all but forgotten six weeks after their decease, so in the case of Mrs. Churchill let us be truthful and rejoice that she can plague her family no more. I presume that life for Mr. C. and Frank C. from now on will take a joyful turn for the better. There should be nothing now to prevent the announcement of the engagement.

Oh, yes, we are still convinced they are engaged while conceding the fact of Miss Fairfax's accepting a post with Mrs. Smallridge is small (pardon, I could not resist) evidence against it. Doubtless there is some explanation. Mr. P. is absolutely certain he is right. As for Frank Churchill's ill-natured comments at Box Hill about an acquaintance formed in a watering place, could it not be a shaft deliberately aimed – a lover's quarrel, in fact?

Mr. P. does not think you can discount the pianoforte whatever other outward circumstances appear to disprove his theory.

We are positive Colonel Campbell did not send it for reasons already put forward. Well, time will reveal all.

We were both extremely interested in what you had to say about Miss Woodhouse and Mr. Knightley. Poor Miss W., with her quick mind, I daresay made a thoughtless remark to Miss Bates without considering how it would be received. I sympathize deeply with her in her distress, because it is just the sort of thing I have often done, myself!

Mr. P. is now well enough to continue the search for a better house. His man of business brings him lists of prospective properties to let. When he is quite recovered we will go out and inspect them together.

It would be more easy to do so, if we had our own carriage. I mentioned to him that even the apothecary at Highbury was thinking of getting one.

"An apothecary, my dear," said he, "is out in all weathers and at all times of night. He has need of a carriage; we do not."

He seems quite determined on the subject. There will be more pounds available for other things, says he, if we do not have a coachman and horses to maintain. He sees no object in *squandering* money, and he considers a carriage in London to be a case in point. Since he is liberal, generous and obliging in most things I have had to give up on the matter.

I am very glad to hear what you have to say about young Charlotte. The long-expected letter from Lieutenant M. has just come at last. Thank goodness. Herewith enclosed. The child will be so happy.

Adieu,

Charlotte

LETTER 59

From Mrs. Goddard to Mrs. Pinkney

Highbury,
30 June 1814

My dear Charlotte,

Well, if the greatest worry you should ever have during the rest of your life is whether to set up, or not to set up, your carriage, you will be a most fortunate woman.

Charlotte's letter, as no doubt she, herself, has or will inform you, is to announce the probable return of Lieutenant Marlowe in August. You will never guess where he has been. In the Mediterranean! Apparently there was some idea that Napoleon might escape from Elba, and his ship was sent down there on that account. She told me with shining eyes that he had written he had something very particular to say to her. Well, it would not be everybody's choice to be the wife of a sailor. Still, she is a sailor's daughter, and must be well aware of the separations and privations. She does seem to be very much in love. Their affection for each other has doubtless been developing through his absence and their correspondence. I hope when they meet again they will not in any way be disappointed.

One piece of information is most promising. With Napoleon on Elba and so many officers being turned ashore, through the interest of the Admiral, he is still to be employed. He is indeed fortunate to have this connexion. I presume it will make the marriage more possible.

The day after the Box Hill picnic, Mr. Knightley left Highbury to spend some time in Brunswick Square. Like Mr. Elton's departure for Bath, it seems a decision hurriedly-taken. There is something queer about it, because I do not believe he likes to be away from home at this time of year when the country is at its best and the crops are growing and needing attention. I wonder if his words with Miss Woodhouse had anything to do with it? Oh, how gossipy I sound. But I never breathe anything of this sort to anyone but you, dear Charlotte.

Harriet is a little low. She tells me that she has often been in company with Mr. Knightley lately and that he has singled her out for attention. This would certainly not have been the case six months ago. She has become very much more self-possessed, and rates herself much more highly than she used to do. Oh, my dear Charlotte, heaven forbid your prognostication that she is likely to be in love with him: a most preposterous and unseemly attachment.

Poor Jane Fairfax (whom you and Mr. Pinkney persist in believing engaged to be married) and who is to leave for Mrs. Smallridge's very shortly, is far from well, suffering from severe headaches. I know Miss Bates is most concerned, and Mrs. Perry tells me Mr. Perry has been to see her and feels that as things are at present, she will not be able to go to her new situation on the date promised. According to Mrs. Perry, Miss Woodhouse has been very kind in offering the carriage for an airing and trying in every way she can to be of use, so relations between herself and Miss Bates must have been patched up, or some apology made or implied; though now I come to think of it, I believe Mrs. Perry said the offer was not accepted.

Lest Mr. Pinkney thinks – for I know he sees these letters, that I have nothing better to do than gossip about my neighbours, I think for my own self-respect and your husband's good opinion, I must tell you some of the vexing questions that I have had to deal with this very day. The father of the two Abbots writes that now there is peace he wishes to take his daughters on a tour to France, and would like them home before the end of the term. I must therefore make arrangements for their travel with adequate chaperones. This will necessitate going to the Crown and speaking to John Abdy to see what can be arranged. I hope I do not run into that scoundrel who was Alice's downfall. I should be so tempted to tell him what I thought of him.

Next, a mother with a delicate daughter came to interview me. If she sent her to the school could she be fed a special diet? Regretfully, I had to turn her down. I have already – in the common phrase – to treat Sarah with "kid gloves." She is such a very good cook, and so much of the contentment among the girls depends on her excellent meals, that I could not possibly risk asking her to prepare particular dishes for a finicky eater when her own cooking is beyond reproach.

My final interview was with the Highbury builder. The roof was leaking last winter – so badly we were obliged to place buckets to catch the drips in many of the attic rooms. So I have asked him to see about mending it during the holidays when the children are gone. You must be prepared for noise and confusion while you are here, dear Charlotte.

Then, today, we have also to begin the lavender bags. The blossoms from the border have been picked, stripped and dried and now the old lavender must be emptied away and the bags filled with fresh. The whole process from start to finish takes considerable time, but the delicious scent in the drawers and the linen cupboard – that lasts all winter – makes the trouble well worthwhile.

These are some of the workaday concerns with which I have to contend, and I am sure you find them a good deal less interesting than the affairs of the Churchills, the Woodhouses, the Westons, the Knightleys and the Bateses.

Ever yours aff:ly,
M. Goddard

LETTER 60

From Mrs. Pinkney to Mrs. Goddard

Sloane Street
London
3 July 1814

You need not concern yourself about Mr. P.'s good opinion, my dear Mary. I can assure you that you have it in full measure. I am sometimes almost jealous of his admiration for you. He can hardly wait to make your acquaintance and wants you to know that he, for one, never imagined that you could run a successful school if all you did was gossip and brood over your neighbours' affairs.

It is probably quite infuriating for you, but I was already aware that the John Knightleys had a visitor. Mr. Wingfield called here and said that the elder brother, Mr. George Knightley, was staying there, and that he seemed low and out of spirits. The children complained to him (Mr. Wingfield) that their uncle would not throw them up to the ceiling and play with them as he usually did.

Yes, Mr. P. and I feel sure that the incident with Miss Woodhouse was the cause of Mr. Knightley coming to town. Since he spends so much time at Hartfield, we conclude he felt a break in that routine was most necessary. How could he continue to call there in a friendly manner after his recent "words" with Miss W.?

Charlotte did write to me about Richard Marlowe's promotion. A great piece of luck for him, which we trust is luck for her, too. That fainting spell on our steps last autumn was the best piece of luck of all. From *that* everything else has come. How fortunate she was to be deprived of breakfast that morning! Mr. P. remarked what strange circumstances, unperceived by us, govern our lives. Presumably, missing that particular breakfast has set her up for breakfasts for the rest of her life.

So, Jane Fairfax is languishing with headaches, is she? Mr. P. assumes, then, that her engagement is still a guilty secret. Is Frank Churchill still flirting with Emma Woodhouse, we wonder?

We have found a house in Hans Place, just around the corner from us. It is on the sunny side, and has a most charming aspect. Several rooms must be painted, however, and we hope that it may be done in August when we are with you. That will give the necessary time to sweeten it.

Not long now, dear Mary, before we actually meet!

Adieu,

Charlotte

LETTER 61

From Mrs. Goddard to Mrs. Pinkney

Highbury,
8 July 1814

My dear Charlotte,

Ten thousand apologies are due to Mr. Pinkney. Jane Fairfax and Frank Churchill are *indeed* engaged, and have been since October. Everything was exactly as he foretold. They are to marry as soon as the mourning period is over and will live at Enscombe.

It is supposed to be a great secret, but Miss Bates, whom I met in Ford's, could not resist whispering the news in my ear. She hinted at misunderstandings, lost letters – not surprising, if Frank Churchill had the posting of them – and lovers' quarrels; exactly as Mr. Pinkney surmised. The gist of it all was that Frank Churchill was obliged to confess his engagement to Mr. Church-ill in order to prevent Jane Fairfax from going off to Mrs. Smallridge's. That is the reason it has been announced *now* so soon after the death of Mrs. Churchill, who, of course, was an insuperable obstacle. Mr. Churchill, apparently, is perfectly amiable and compliant. Needless to say, the proposal of going to Mrs. Smallridge is abandoned.

The dear Bateses are delighted, and no doubt this is the restorative needed to rid Miss Fairfax of her headaches. She has evidently been through a most trying time and very much felt the evil of this secret engagement and the deception they have been practising on others, much more so than *him*, I believe. *He* was, if anything, diverted by the artifice; while *she* was ashamed of the dishonesty of thus imposing on their friends.

But you have gathered from my letters, what sort of young man he is: not one to be incommoded by the strictest principles of right and wrong. He is extremely fortunate to have secured the affections of such an upright young woman. Heaven knows one wishes them happy, and hopes that the probity of her character may amend the flaws in his.

Harriet has just come in from Hartfield. She met Mr. Weston in her way there and he told her the news, since he said Miss Woodhouse already knew, she might as well know also. Not such a secret, after all, it seems.

Harriet was quite taken by the affair. "Oh, Mrs. Goddard," she kept repeating, "is not this the oddest news that ever was?" Apart from the oddity of it, the affair did not appear to discompose her, she was merely struck, as we all were – except Mr. Pinkney – by the unexpectedness of it. So she cannot be in love with Frank Churchill, at least. I sincerely hope it is not Mr. Knightley. That would be too absurd.

July 9th. I was prevented from sealing this, and now I have something more to add. I asked Harriet this morning what time she was leaving for Hartfield, as I wanted to give her a pattern to be matched at Ford's, which she would be passing on her way. Harriet said that she would be glad to leave the pattern when she went for her walk, but she was not going to Hartfield for the next while. Surprised, I inquired if Miss Woodhouse were unwell.

Harriet looked a little conscious as she replied that Miss Woodhouse was quite well, but she, Harriet, felt that she had been too little at home lately. She was going to tidy her drawers and mend her stockings.

Tidy her drawers! Instead of visit her friend! I could hardly believe my ears. It is the first time since she was ill at Christmas that Harriet has not gone to Hartfield. She must have had some disagreement with Miss Woodhouse: a very serious matter for Harriet, since she has so imprudently given up her friendship with the Martins.

She was obviously unwilling to say more, so I suggested she leave the drawers for now, and since it was such a fine day she and Miss Bickerton might include Charlotte in their walk. As the three girls set off, I said partly in jest, "Look out for gypsies!" I knew I was perfectly safe since Mr. Knightley had made sure the band had left the neighbourhood. Charlotte, and even Miss Bickerton, laughed, but the reference seemed to pain Harriet, who said, please, do not remind her.

Strange. Off they went and I can speculate no further. I suppose you and Mr. Pinkney can easily solve that riddle?

Ever yours,

M. Goddard

LETTER 62

From Mrs. Pinkney to Mrs. Goddard

Sloane Street
London
10 July 1814

My dear Mary,

Mr. Pinkney is highly gratified that his prognostications proved accurate. It is always pleasant to be right! Whatever would

Mrs. Churchill have said? If she is looking down upon us, she must be struck by how remarkably soon after her death the way was made plain for the young people. Poor Miss Fairfax. One understands how she must have felt. How she must have hated the deception! Well, now she will be rewarded by a comfortable income and a young man she loves.

Speaking of love, Mr. P. says he cannot conceive why Harriet Smith should not be going to Hartfield, or whom she may be in love with at *this* particular moment. Frankly, he is rather bored with that young woman. He thinks Jane Fairfax and Miss Woodhouse are much more interesting characters.

Mr. Wingfield has just called. He tells me that Harriet is now at Brunswick Square: playing musical chairs, it seems, with Mr. Knightley who has gone back to Highbury. This is a new development, is it not? We wonder if there is some connexion, both being intimate friends of Miss Woodhouse? Or perhaps I should say both *were* intimate friends of Miss W.

Well, we shall soon be in Highbury ourselves. Then all these names will become faces and people to us. How much we look forward to that.

Meanwhile, we visit our new house in Hans Place and I measure for curtains and carpets. Our daily walk, we have resumed. The port decanter is put away indefinitely. I order only simple meals, though we have not yet sunk to the level of Mr. Woodhouse's basin of gruel. But, in spite of this abstention from good food and drink, we are both very cheerful, dear Mary, and much occupied with plans for our move. The servants, also, are rejoiced. They did not like this house, either.

Charlotte writes affectionately and is full of your kindness. She enjoyed her half holiday walking with the two parlour boarders: much girlish chat, apparently, about what sort of husbands they might get, and though Miss Bickerton and Harriet hinted that the men of their choice were in Highbury. (Who?) Charlotte, is, I imagine, the most likely of the three to marry soon; she told me that although they asked her, she gave nothing away.

I suppose she is mindful, poor child, from bitter experience, that when it comes to the navy there's "many a slip 'twixt cup and lip." Lieutenant Marlowe is back in the Channel in one of the seventeen ships chasing the American schooner *Neufchatel*. Those Yankees certainly give our ships a run for their money! I suppose, with that name, they must have captured her from the French.

My dear Mary, a miracle! The unimaginable has happened. Betty just came in and handed me an express from Admiral Seymour. Some shipwrecked sailors have been discovered on an island off the coast of South America: among them, Charlotte's father! Pray inform Charlotte, give her my love and tell her that I shall write to the Admiral with her address. He can then communicate future developments directly. The intelligence was brought to England by a fast cutter. Captain Gordon and his crew are on their way home in a slower vessel.

Adieu,

Charlotte

LETTER 63

From Mrs. Goddard to Mrs. Pinkney

Highbury,
15 July 1814

You should have seen young Charlotte's face when I gave her the news. At first, disbelief, then wonder, and finally complete and utter joy. "Oh, Mrs. Goddard," cried she, "I hardly know how to bear such happiness." Fortune does seem to have smiled on the child. Gratifying to think that there is some justice, that Providence can be merciful in dealing with one who has endured so much misery and privation.

Well, my dear Charlotte, how extraordinary you seem to know what goes on in Highbury almost before I do, myself. Yes, Harriet went up to Brunswick Square. She had a tooth which needed attention, and Miss Woodhouse kindly arranged this invitation for her. I must have been mistaken in assuming there was some coolness between them. Mr. Woodhouse's carriage conveyed her thither, so she went quite in style. She has not been in London before, and I am sure the novelty will improve the low spirits which seem to have affected her lately.

With reference to these nameless men you speak of, who live in Highbury, that she and Miss Bickerton aspire to – I would really rather *not* know these things.

As for Mr. Pinkney finding Miss Woodhouse and Miss Fairfax more interesting – they certainly are more *elegant* and worldly young women than my little Harriet. But you must be aware that the interest I take in her affairs is that of a mother. For Emma Woodhouse and Jane Fairfax I can do nothing; for Harriet, everything. Of course she is a simple girl, and easily swayed. But with her affectionate disposition and good temper, with the right man she will make a very contented wife. Can one say that of either of the other two? Does superior intellect and accomplishment necessarily assume the possession of that great gift of being always happy? – a quality which I think it is not wise to scorn. But I get too near to moralizing.

I have to announce with pleasure Mrs. Weston's safety with a little girl. It is to be named after herself, Anna. My Alice had her child two weeks ago, also a girl. She is calling it Mary, after me. I am to be godmother. I hope she may be back with me again by next term, or Christmas at the latest. Do not feel that this means that I shall no longer require Charlotte. She is useful and agreeable and I am happy to keep her as long as she wishes to stay.

The school year is drawing to a close. I confess I am tired and shall be glad of a rest. My triumph this past year has been little Sukey, who now laughs and runs about and rolls down the green slope in the lawn with the best of them. This gives me the greatest possible satisfaction. If only I had succeeded in bringing about the marriage of Harriet Smith and Robert Martin, I should be entirely content. *That* I must account one of my failures.

How I anticipate your visit, my dearest Charlotte.

Ever yours,
Mary

P.S. Frank Churchill and Miss Fairfax have offered me the famous pianoforte. It is not worthwhile transporting to Enscombe where there are two instruments already. Am I not fortunate? It shall be kept for the older and best pupils.

LETTER 64

From Mrs. Pinkney to Mrs. Goddard

Sloane Street
London
20 July 1814

Well, my dear Mary, your letter was full of good news. Both Mrs. Weston and Alice safe! At their age, childbed is such a hazardous undertaking: I am exceedingly relieved that all is well.

I speak with particular feeling, from the bottom of my heart in fact. Can you not guess why? Prepare youself, my dear Mary, impossible as it may seem, I, too, am to be a mother. Mr. Wingfield confirmed my worst suspicions a few days ago. About next Valentine's Day is the date he hazards for my *accouchement*. I could not write to you sooner. I had first to compose myself, and that took some doing, you may be sure.

Mr. Pinkney, of course, is overjoyed. I say to him, "It is all very well for *you*. I am far too old to have a child, and, besides, I have never cared for children." "Oh," says he with the greatest good humour in the world, "but you will care for your own. Mothers always do." Luckily, I am very well, though extremely apprehensive. But after the initial shock I do not say too much. Mr. Pinkney is so delightfully happy, so solicitous and affection-ate, that I cannot in good conscience diminish his pleasure. "To think, I may have a son!" he cries. "I never thought it would happen, my dearest, dearest Charlotte. What a gift you have given me." You may imagine what reply I might have made to this effusion, but I refrained. Dear Mr. Pinkney. His joy is quite marvellous to behold. He has a permanent smile affixed to his face and I hear him singing to himself as he goes about the house. Since I am perfectly well, I can make no complaint, except the dread of the Event itself which even now, seven months ahead, haunts me. Mr. Wingfield does his best to allay my fears, telling me of various mothers he has known who were about my age when they were successfully delivered of their first child.

Although I can think of little else, I must answer your letter, because you know I am and have been most interested in all you tell me of Highbury. In my opinion your success with little Sukey is a far more important achievement than arranging a match between Harriet and Robert Martin. They are not children, they can be left to manage their own affairs. You undertake too much, dear Mary. I can well see you in eleven or twelve years' time lamenting over an unprosperous courtship for Sukey.

It is most fitting that you should have Miss Fairfax's pianoforte. No one, I am sure, could make better use of it. At first, I was surprised that she could bring herself to part with her Valentine's Day present; but then, as Mr. P. points out, perhaps she views it as an unpleasant relic from a vexatious period of her life. She would rather *not* have it within sight to remind her of a time of deceit and double-dealing.

I knew young Charlotte would suit, and am pleased that you will keep her on if necessary. That brings me to a favour I have to ask you. Charlotte writes that Richard Marlowe will be here on leave during August. She wonders how and where she can see him. She is reluctant to appeal to you herself, but since the school will be empty of girls, and we will all be there, is it possible that he could stay with you? What do you think? If it is an imposition, do say so; but at least, with all of us present, they will be very adequately chaperoned!

If it is not convenient, Mr. P. says we could accommodate them both for a short time in our new house when we remove to it. At present there is plenty of room. Once the child arrives, and its nurse, I may not be so free with my invitations.

Yours,

Charlotte

LETTER 65

From Mrs. Goddard to Mrs. Pinkney

Highbury,
21 July 1814

My dearest, dearest Charlotte,

What splendid, splendid news! I was obliged to read your letter two or three times over before I could believe the words before my eyes. Congratulations, indeed, my dear. I cannot tell you how delighted I am for you and Mr. Pinkney. I give you fair warning. I intend to be a most devoted aunt. Aunts are very important, you know. They can be more indulgent than mere mothers.

Now, as your older sister, who has been through several confinements herself, I beg that you will not fret and worry and be fearful for the next seven months. You will only make yourself and Mr. Pinkney miserable. You are very healthy and strong. Consider the happy outcome of Mrs. Weston and Alice and expect the same for yourself. Rejoice in your condition. This will prove to be the beginning of a new era in your life, one that promises greater happiness than ever before. Although I would not wish to deny Mr. Pinkney his boy, I must say that I should relish a girl for you and for myself. A girl would be such a companion and friend. And although she will not be obliged, like a boy, to be sent away to school, who knows that when she is twelve or thirteen you might be very glad to have her out of the way for a while and let her scramble herself into a little education in Highbury.

Now to turn to more mundane matters. Yes, of course Richard Marlowe may stay at the school. The girls have left and there are empty bedrooms and to spare. Heaven knows I am happy to promote the felicity of all young couples. It will be good for the young people to be together here with us, in what you might call a domestic situation – a situation more like day-to-day living than their previous experience of dashing about in carriages as they did at Bath: rather too much like the acquaintance "formed at a watering place" so reprobated by Frank Churchill at the Box Hill picnic of evil memory.

Young Charlotte needs to remove her head out of the clouds, I believe. As a matter of a fact I was down in the kitchen earlier today to see how Sarah and the maids were getting on with the jam-making. Owing to the good weather, the fruit is excellent this year. Charlotte happened to be passing through on some errand at the time, and had eyes as big as saucers. She said she had never seen so many rows of jars laid out in one place before.

"But, Charlotte," said I, "there are a great many people here to eat them. When you are married, jam-making will be one of the tasks that will require your supervision." She looked quite taken aback. I had to laugh. I suppose like most young people she imagines they can live on love and air. I must ask Sarah to give her some cooking lessons when the last of the girls have left and she is more at leisure.

Goodness me, how trifling and dull are these bits and pieces compared to your momentous news.

I am pleased to report that Harriet is writing more cheerfully from Brunswick Square. She is beginning to enjoy London. Mrs. John Knightley is very kind, and Harriet is happy to play with the children. I conclude she has made herself very agreeable which must account for her being invited to stay longer than originally planned.

Good Heavens, my dear Charlotte, I was interrupted by the Bateses' Patty bringing a note from Miss Bates. The most astounding news! You will never guess who is engaged to be married: Mr. Knightley and Miss Woodhouse! I am completely taken by surprise. Yet it is so natural, so proper, so suitable, I wonder none of us ever thought of it before. Not even your clever husband? I, for one, would never have considered it a possibility after what Harriet told me of the episode at Box Hill:

Mr. Knightley reproving Miss Woodhouse and she in tears! Yet, if one considers the event more carefully, plainly one does not reprove someone for their behavior if one is indifferent. Evidentally Mr. Knightley cared very much that Miss Woodhouse should speak so cruelly to Miss Bates, and Emma equally must have been distressed at forfeiting his good opinion of her.

Well, I will not weary you with more. Here is John come to take this letter to the post office. I am anxious that there should be no delay, and that you and Mr. Pinkney should receive my most affectionate congratulations as soon as possible.

Your proud and loving sister,
Mary

P.S. With this most interesting news I look forward to your visit with even greater anticipation. So much as we will have to talk about! I wonder if you have thought of any names yet?

LETTER 65, cont.

From Mrs. Goddard to Mrs. Pinkney

I cannot forbear writing to you again, my dear Charlotte, and I trust you will not mind the expense of two letters from me on the same day, but I felt that I must send you a few lines to say that no sooner had my previous letter been safely taken off by John than Mrs. Perry called.

I hope you will not feel I have betrayed your confidence when I confess that I told her your news. She is discretion itself, accustomed to giving nothing away, being the wife of Mr. Perry. (I would not, for example, dream of uttering a word to Miss Bates, or, for that matter to Charlotte. It is for you to tell her if and when you choose.) But my head is so full of you and I am so happy at the prospect of your having a child, and Mrs. Perry is such a good old friend, that I could not resist confiding in her. She was warmly congratulatory, and told me of various patients of Mr.

173

Perry who, while not quite young, had had perfectly safe and satisfactory confinements. He recommends exercise and moderation in eating and drinking. But that is just what you have been doing for Mr. Pinkney's gout, is it not?

After we had very thoroughly discussed your interesting condition, of course we moved on to the engagement of Mr. Knightley and Emma Woodhouse. You will be amused to hear that the difficulty of what to do with Mr. Woodhouse has been resolved. Mr. Knightley proposes to leave Donwell Abbey and is going to live at Hartfield! Poor William Larkins. I do not know how he will take such a change. Mrs. Perry tells me there is much gossip about this unusual arrangement. Mrs. Elton is the most scornful: it will never do. She knew some people near Maple Grove who had tried it, etc., etc.

Speculation is rife as to what will become of Mr. Knightley's house and servants. Some think he should rent Donwell until such time as Mr. Woodhouse dies, others that he should turn it over to the John Knightleys. Still others suggest that he should keep William Larkins on, and walk to Donwell daily from Hartfield as he has been accustomed in the past to walk every day to Hartfield from Donwell.

My own idea is that he should ask Robert Martin to supervise the place for him. He must be very much in love to make such a sacrifice of his own house and independence. A definite date for the wedding has not yet been set. I imagine dear old Mr. Woodhouse must be given time to become accustomed to the idea.

Yours affectionately,

M. Goddard

LETTER 66

From Mrs. Pinkney to Mrs. Goddard

Sloane Street
London
23 July 1814

I am glad you are pleased, my dear Mary. I confess that with each day that passes I become more reconciled to my situation. I have discovered a noteworthy fact: a pregnant woman becomes very important, more important than she has ever been before, not only in her own eyes, but in those of the people around her. Mr. Pinkney keeps begging me to *rest*. "Mr. Pinkney," say I, "I am not an invalid. Every single person that you observe in the street outside this house was born and has a mother." (I am a little amused at myself, taking up this position that it is all in the course of nature, for in truth, I am still very apprehensive.)

If it gives you pleasure to have told Mrs. Perry, I will not object. I should only complain if the whole of Highbury were to be informed, but if Mrs. Perry is as discreet as you say, then I have nothing to fear. I will tell Charlotte, myself, when I come. Good Heavens, it has just occurred to me that if she marries soon, we may both be with child together. There's a thought to conjure with!

Please, dear Mary, do not leap so far ahead into the future as to plan the entry of this unborn *boy* into your school already.

But enough of me and my child when you have such very remarkable news in Highbury.

No, indeed, Mr. Pinkney did *not* guess that Miss Woodhouse and Mr. Knightley were forming an attachment. He suspects it came upon *her* unawares, and that *his* sudden departure for Brunswick Square was somehow instrumental in bringing it about. So

175

much for Emma Woodhouse declaring she would never marry. I, for one, never believed it.

As you say he must be very much in love to surrender his own home and independence. Mr. P. says he admires him, *indeed*. To be a permanent guest in another man's house, to put up with Mr. Woodhouse each and every day – not for me, thank you, says Mr. P. He observes that only a man of the strongest character, only a man absolutely secure and established in his own person would have the courage to embark on such an arrangement. We think your "dear old Mr. Woodhouse" must be excessively selfish to accept this sacrifice. We suppose he is unable to realize anything beyond his own comfort, and is so wrapped up in himself as to be quite unaware of the feelings of others.

The painters are hard at work in the new house. Mr. Pinkney is so very concerned that the smell of paint might affect his *son* that he will barely allow me to stick my nose inside the door.

I have been occupying myself by packing such small things as fine linen and the best china and must trust Charles and Betty to manage the rest during our absence in Highbury.

Only a few more days and we shall be there!

Adieu,

Charlotte

LETTER 67

From Mrs. Goddard to Mrs. Pinkney

Highbury,
28 July 1814

More splendid news, my dear Charlotte. Robert Martin marries Harriet Smith!

It seems too miraculous for words. I had a note from Harriet yesterday. She sounded extremely happy. But I could hardly have believed it if Robert Martin, himself, had not called here this morning. Of course I congratulated him most warmly, and told him many pleasing little anecdotes about Harriet as a child. Lover-like, he quite hung upon my words.

The purpose of his visit, however, was to ask particulars of her parentage. I told him about her father, and assured him that I knew he would treat him most liberally. I have now written to that good man to apprise him of the news. He will be delighted. I know he has been concerned about Harriet's future.

You will wonder how this all came about, since Harriet is still in Brunswick Square. Robert Martin was up in town for a few days on business. He was delivering papers to Mr. John Knightley from his brother, and was invited to join their family party for the evening. They had tickets to Astley's apparently. Robert Martin said that, at the time, Harriet was very nervous of the performing horses and the great crowds, and while John Knightley took charge of Mrs. Knightley and little Henry, he shepherded Harriet and little John. The consequence of this adventure – together with another invitation to dine at Brunswick Square the following day—was this engagement. Harriet has always been partial to him, and being away from Highbury, I can only assume, made her see matters in their proper light, and she came to her senses at last. Whatever may have been the cause, the result is most satisfactory: what a happy conclusion to all my worries.

Harriet is to stay on with the Knightleys until they come down for their holiday in August. They plan a lengthy visit to Hartfield, apparently.

After Robert Martin left, I immediately sent a few lines to Mrs. Martin expressing my great joy. Her reply is just come. She does not wax quite so enthusiastic as I would wish. But it is only natural, I suppose, remembering the events of last year. She must have wondered, as a mother would, how any girl could refuse her excellent son. As for me, it is the culmination of the past ten years in which I have been bringing up Harriet with just some such happy end in view.

Your delighted and most affectionate sister,
Mary

P.S. I see that I neglected to comment on your remarks about Mr. Woodhouse. If you knew him, you would understand that no other arrangement is even remotely possible. I am sure Mr. Knightley and Miss Woodhouse will manage him admirably, as they have always done in the past. Hartfield is a large house. They will certainly be able to achieve a measure of privacy.

LETTER 68

From Mrs. Pinkney to Mrs. Goddard

Sloane Street
London
30 July 1814

Well! A visit to Brunswick Square seems to be highly efficacious in promoting suitable engagements.

Yes, my dear Mary, given my propensity for knowing Highbury news almost before you do, you will not be surprised to learn that I had a hint from Mr. Wingfield about Harriet.

He said he was called to Brunswick Square the day after they had been to Astley's to attend Mrs. J. K. She was suffering a nervous spell in consequence of the great crowd in which they had been caught the previous evening. Mr. Wingfield was there just before dinner, and noticed a rather countrified young man hovering attentively around Harriet and her evident pleasure in his company. I asked who this could have been? Mr. Wingfield said that although he had not been introduced, he understood he was from Highbury. Mr. P. and I surmised that it could be none other than Robert Martin.

Be all that as it may, I am delighted for your sake, my dear Mary, though I do wonder about the stability of Harriet Smith's affections. She certainly was in love with Mr. Elton, and who knows with whom else, besides.

Mr. Wingfield came here to say goodbye and to admonish us when we go to Highbury to stick to the regimen that has answered so well, though remarking that at a *school* he imagined there was not much temptation to over-indulge in good food. I promptly set him right about *that*. He begged my pardon, and went on to say he imagined I might meet the John Knightleys as they were going for their holiday to the same place. I hope we become intimate. I should very much like to seek Mrs. Knightley's advice (she, the mother of five) on confinements and nursing. Since we share the same apothecary, I do not think it would be at all improper.

Just fancy, soon, all these inimitable Highbury people who are at present only names we shall be able to meet in person. But the most important of all is *you*, my dear Mary – after nearly seventeen years! What will we think of each other? Will we be a little shy, at first? Then young Charlotte and her Richard will be there. I do look forward to seeing them both again; a real family party under your hospitable roof.

Best love, yours ever
Charlotte

LETTER 69

From Mrs. Goddard to Mrs. Pinkney

Highbury
1 August 1814

My dear Charlotte,

I have no fears for the marriage of Harriet Smith and Robert Martin. She will doubtless become the mother of a large family, and in due course will be measuring her own little boys and girls against the very wainscot where Robert Martin – as she once told me measured himself and his sisters. She will be happy and busy.

Even as Jane Fairfax is superior to Frank Churchill, so Robert Martin's sterling worth cannot fail to foster steadiness and respectability in Harriet. The same is true of Mr. Knightley and Emma Woodhouse. I suppose no match can ever be uniformly equal. One spouse must always be superior to the other.

No, dear Charlotte, I do not feel either of us will be at all shy when we meet. If anyone might feel a little diffident, I should think it might be Mr. Pinkney, caught between two sisters, who, I daresay, will never stop talking for the entire month of August.

You will think there is something contagious about love in Highbury. I am almost ashamed to write and tell you of yet *another* engagement; but I have just heard of one more. I really believe this will positively be the last.

Miss Bickerton walked in while I was beginning this letter and announced she is to marry the old writing master's son. For *her*, plain, dull and without prospects, it is a perfectly eligible connexion. So your fears are for nothing, dear Charlotte. No old spinsters of seventeen and eighteen for me. I am rid of both my parlour boarders and shall have to look for others, that is, if I am ever to buy my little cottage and retire.

Your rooms are ready: the beds aired, the furniture polished with beeswax and fresh lavender placed in the drawers. Young Charlotte cannot sit still and keeps begging me to find occupation for her. She is counting the hours until Lieutenant Marlowe and you and Mr. Pinkney appear; or perhaps I should put that the other way round: he is actually arriving two or three days after you, which I am glad of. It will give us time to talk and for you to settle in before we have this additional distraction.

Only three days left until I see you both. *How* I look forward to it.

Your most affectionate sister,
Mary

LETTER 70

From Mrs. Pinkney to Mrs. Goddard

Sloane Street
London
3 August 1814

Finally, finally, we are to meet, my dearest Mary. Although I shall see you tomorrow, I had to send these few lines: the last I shall be writing to you for a whole month. I will be quite at a loss without my pen and my writing desk. But how blissful it will be to be able to speak to you directly whenever I have something to say instead of storing it up to 'write to Mary.'

I was looking through your letters last night, and reading how you sent a note to Miss Woodhouse in October and asked if you might bring Harriet Smith to Hartfield. Is there any reason why you could not propose introducing your sister and brother-in-law, likewise? I know I will never meet Mr. Woodhouse in the street, and I quite long to be acquainted with him and Emma and Mr. Knightley. The inside of Hartfield, too, I would very much like to see; I might get some ideas for the fitting-up of our own new house.

I have just communicated these thoughts to Mr. P. It occurs to *him*, (who is over-scrupulous in these matters in my opinion, but still I must respect his wishes) that you might think it would be a breach of propriety to procure such an invitation for us.

Mr. P. says that Miss Woodhouse may be occupied in soothing and consoling her father; that Mrs. Weston must be busy with her baby; that Miss Bates is likely to be fussing over wedding plans for Miss Fairfax; and that none of them will care a fig about meeting strangers at this time. If this is so, pray do not trouble yourself, we would not want to push ourselves forward like Mrs.

Elton (who may, or, who may not, recognize me as it suits her, but I do not feel anxious to renew *that* acquaintance).

No, if necessary, we will be content to glimpse all these good people at a distance in the High Street, in Ford's, and at church; because if that is what you think best, we would not wish to discommode you for the world.

Lovely, airy Highbury! I am in such a fever of impatience I watch the clock all day, and can hardly wait for tomorrow and the hour of setting off. Until then, and in the greatest anticipation, I am,

Ever your most happy and affectionate sister,
Charlotte